'Why are you here, Gianni?'

'Why?' He tried to understand her mood. The mixed signals she sent and the emotions in her blue eyes. He realised that reading unspoken sentiment from women was not something he was skilled at. 'Because something is wrong. Why are you afraid of seeing me? Talking to me? Afraid of me?'

She lifted her hand and held her throat. 'I'm not afraid of you, Gianni. At times when I'm with you I feel the safest I've ever felt.'

His breath eased out. He'd been unaware he held it as he waited. It was amazing how good that admission made him feel. Perhaps dangerously so. 'Then what is the matter between us?'

He could read the struggle in her eyes and the indecision that crossed her face, but not the cause. Then she said it, baldly, and it was the last thing he'd expected.

'I'm pregnant.'

Mills & Boon® Medical™ Romance
is proud to return to Lyrebird Lake!

Fiona McArthur brings you a fresh instalment
from her fabulous mini-series…

LYREBIRD LAKE MATERNITY

Every day brings a miracle…

It's time for these midwives
to become mothers themselves!

Previously we met Montana, Misty and Mia

'Thank you, Ms McArthur, for a thoroughly enjoyable time spent in your world of Lyrebird Lake, and I can't wait to read of your many more delightful characters too.'
—Cataromance.com

Now it's time to meet Emma.

You'll love her as much as everyone else in Lyrebird Lake!

MIDWIFE IN THE FAMILY WAY

BY

FIONA McARTHUR

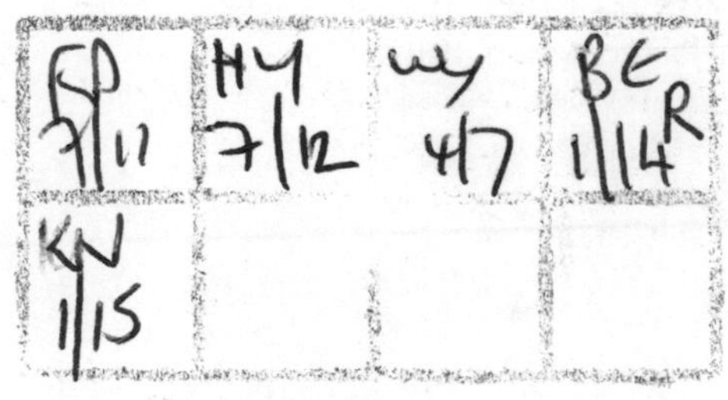

All the characters in this book have no existence outside the imagination of the author, and have no relation whatsoever to anyone bearing the same name or names. They are not even distantly inspired by any individual known or unknown to the author, and all the incidents are pure invention.

First published in Great Britain 2010
Large Print edition 2011
Harlequin Mills & Boon Limited,
Eton House, 18-24 Paradise Road,
Richmond, Surrey TW9 1SR

ISBN: 978 0 263 21732 2

Harlequin Mills & Boon policy is to use papers that are natural, renewable and recyclable products and made from wood grown in sustainable forests. The logging and manufacturing process conform to the legal environmental regulations of the country of origin.

Printed and bound in Great Britain
by CPI Antony Rowe, Chippenham, Wiltshire

A mother to five sons, **Fiona McArthur** is an Australian midwife who loves to write. Medical™ Romance gives Fiona the scope to write about all the wonderful aspects of adventure, romance, medicine and midwifery that she feels so passionate about—as well as an excuse to travel! Now that her boys are older, Fiona and her husband Ian are off to meet new people, see new places, and have wonderful adventures. Fiona's website is at www.fionamcarthur.com

Recent titles by the same author:

THE MIDWIFE AND THE MILLIONAIRE
MIDWIFE IN A MILLION
PREGNANT MIDWIFE: FATHER NEEDED*
THE MIDWIFE'S NEW-FOUND FAMILY*

**Lyrebird Lake Maternity*

Dedicated to my dear friend Michelle.
One of the coolest, bravest,
most amazing people I know,
and whose journey has been my inspiration.
And, like all people with and without the
gene, who have been affected by or known
those affected by Huntington's Disease,
I pray for a cure.

CHAPTER ONE

GIANNI BONMARITO stood isolated and imperious at the edge of the garden and watched an extended family embrace life—at a funeral. While the upbeat emotion on display made his neck itch, he couldn't help but envy the warmth of the mourners.

But, then, everything in this country was warm. Even the ridiculous Queensland sun beat into the darkness inside his head. He watched innocent toddlers wrestle like puppies in the grass, while older, lanky teenagers played back-yard cricket on the lawn with adults. And women laughed. At a funeral?

What place was this? This country outpost hours from Brisbane? A whole town nestled beside a mirrored lake ringed in trees. A small community so close that only first names were used.

The weatherboard doctor's surgery opposite Lyrebird Lake Hospital hosted a wake unlike any he'd seen and the enthusiastic if discordant bagpipes being played by the man he'd come to support was another bizarre example of it.

'Gianni, isn't it?' The blonde came only to his shoulder, trim and tiny, with a spring in her step that captured his attention and shamelessly proclaimed that this woman loved life.

He could barely remember himself like that. She had the most provocative smile he'd seen for a long time, and the most peculiar thing was that when she smiled at him, mysteriously she lifted the pall of darkncss within him as if her fingers held daybreak.

As if she'd tied his troubles to one of those helium balloons the family had let go at the graveside earlier that afternoon. Whoosh.

Gloominess soared away—but physical awareness settled like a hot bowl of liquid in his belly and reminded him what a fool his libido could make of him.

'*Si*. Gianni.'

She smiled again, no doubt at his accent, so strange in this place of vowels. Incredible, Gianni thought, and struggled not to look at her delightful breasts and slim little waist he could have spanned with his fingers. Startled by the first genuine admiration of a woman since his faith in women had shattered for ever, that realisation sent the familiar wave of coldness through his consciousness. How could he trust that feeling?

He reefed his disobedient eyes away from her body to scan her face for a sign of deceit but there was none he could see. He had to stop expecting it.

The sun glinted off the iridescent pink lip gloss she wore, which shone with an exuberantly vibrant colour. Strange choice for a funeral, his clinical brain noted, and he had to be content with that, because nothing else remotely offended.

Mischievous blue eyes scanned his length as openly as he'd scanned hers, and he frowned as his neck heated. What was this? Tangled glances with women did not perturb him. The very idea made no sense.

'I'm sorry.' His voice came out less cordially than he'd intended and the vibration deep in his gut echoed in spirals of awareness he didn't want—and denied adamantly. 'I don't believe we've met or I would have remembered.'

'Emma Rose.' She smiled. 'I'm a friend of the family and one of the midwives at the birth centre.'

He looked from her to the child he only then realised stood beside her, almost as tall in height, hinting at future beauty but surely too young to have reached double figures. 'Your daughter?' The mother looked a child herself.

Emma cast a proud glance at the fair-haired poppy at her side. 'Yes, my daughter. Grace. This is Dr Angus's friend from Italy.' Her voice lowered. 'Dr…?'

'Bonmarito.'

'Hello, Dr Bon-mar-ito.' Grace said carefully as she held out her small hand. She didn't smile. 'A doctor. That's nice.' Somehow Gianni felt a little boring as he took those tiny fingers in his big hand. Little girls were so fragile and made him aware of how much he didn't know about children. Made him remember his wife had been pregnant when she'd died.

'When I grow up I'll be a midwife, like Mum,' Grace stated in a small, determined voice.

Gianni blinked. Even with his limited exposure he could see she was incredibly assured for a young child. Like her mother.

At this child's age Gianni had been interested

in a rocket ship and moon walks, or Formula One racing. Life had been carefree then, before his father and mother had died, and unlike his brother he hadn't been sure he would be a doctor. But then he hadn't known about the realities of life, or near death, hadn't even met Angus.

He shook Grace's hand seriously and exerted himself to be less formal, less pompous around children, which he'd been accused of before. But when had he had the chance to learn? The nearest he'd been to fatherhood had been another man's child that had died with his wife.

He swallowed the familiar bitterness and forced a smile. 'Hello, Grace. You must call me Gianni, as everyone seems to be on first names here.'

As the little girl took her hand back he noted the she had the same vibrant lip gloss on as her mother. Perhaps a family make-up party? He tried not to grimace at the idea of frivolity in a time of grief. Not something he was used to but, then, everything seemed different here. Even himself.

'Your lipstick matches your mother's.' He looked back at Emma and the thrum in his belly growled louder, like a sleeping beast he seemed unable to control.

Now her blue eyes had softened compassionately as she concentrated on his face and he found himself drawn into her gaze, unable to break the connection.

When she said, 'Ned bought that lip gloss for my daughter for Christmas, and we wore it today to honour him,' Gianni sighed internally. He'd been wrong there, too.

Still she drew him in like a siren. Such sympathy, such warmth and promise of healing as he'd never felt before, as if she recognised his pain and shared the ache. Like the peace inside a tiny church on an Italian hillside.

He dragged his eyes away from her to her daughter. Ridiculous feelings needed to be ignored. Especially ones that left him floundering for composure.

'No school today, Grace?'

Grace looked suitably downcast for a second as the reason they were there returned to her. He watched, annoyed with himself for the obvious question and the distress it had caused. Children brought out the worst in him, and he wanted to walk away and save them from his gaucheness, but he couldn't.

The little girl forced herself to smile and explain. 'It's Ned Day. The school shut for Dr Ned's "happy" wake.'

Emma rested one elegant hand on her daughter's shoulder. 'We all loved Ned. It must feel different for someone from another country. Funerals can be celebrations as well as sad events in different cultures, Grace.' She smiled again at Gianni. 'Ned said we had to celebrate life, not be maudlin at its natural conclusion. Hence the children and the balloons.' She gestured to the youngsters playing on the grass. 'And the backyard cricket.'

He glanced at Angus, Ned's son and his friend, the man who had pulled him many years ago from the earthquake debris when all others had given up. The man who had turned Gianni from a thoughtless playboy bent on self-destruction into a dedicated medic.

To be honest, Angus perplexed him, too. Gianni didn't understand why Angus smiled as he struggled with the bagpipes he hadn't mastered fully before his father had died. But, then, surely the fact that Angus could smile was a thing to feel relieved about.

Apparently this place was not for gravity and ceremony. He wished he'd met the man who inspired such warmth and feeling of life even after he'd gone. Perhaps he, Gianni, had needed somewhere like this in his grief because it felt he'd been in the darkness for such a long time.

Emma too looked across at Ned's son. 'Angus

told me you lost your wife.' He winced at the memory of all that had happened that day but then she leaned forward and kissed his cheek in unselfconscious sympathy. 'I am sorry to hear that.'

The scent of strawberries hung on his face where she'd brushed her lips and he could feel the breeze on the exact spot, fanning the heat from her mouth.

In all his life strawberries had never caused such upheaval! Why had she kissed him? Though, when her blue eyes softened even more with empathy, it was strangely acceptable.

'And now,' she went on, 'you've come to be with Angus for his loss. That's kind. He'll miss Ned, sorely.'

He dragged his mind back to her words and couldn't believe how disorientated his usually clinical mind had become since she'd arrived beside him. 'Thank you. I regret I didn't come in time to meet Dr Campbell.'

'He was a kind man, too.' Her hand lifted and with one gentle fingertip she wiped the trace of colour from his cheek. 'Oops. Sorry.'

'It smells very nice,' he said, and allowed himself another slow glance at her mouth, unobtrusively. No law against that, and he imagined what her lips would taste like. Where was his brain going? To a place it hadn't been for a long time. He needed to stop these fantasies. 'Perhaps you would like to introduce me to your husband?'

She tilted her head and he saw the second she mentally stepped back. 'No husband.'

'A widow perhaps, or divorced?' She shook her head with a mocking little smile that made him want to taste her even more.

He was too interested in the facts. Looking for a reason not to be drawn to her. She must have been very young when her daughter had been born. Too young to be a mother and not the child herself. Whose fault was it she was not protected?

'None of those.' She didn't elaborate. He felt rather than saw the wall go up. Her expression remained friendly but there was a more assertive tilt to her delightful chin that dared him to judge. This woman had him far too intrigued for a man who would be leaving tomorrow.

He persisted. 'Your parents are here?'

'My parents don't live in Lyrebird Lake any more.' She lifted her chin higher. 'Have you any children?' Her turn to question.

Not of his own. And never would. 'No.'

She lifted an ironic eyebrow and glanced down at Grace, and the subject spluttered out like a candle in the rain.

From the gate a dark-haired girl of about Grace's age waved at them and Emma touched her daughter's shoulder until she saw her friend. Emma nodded. 'There's Dawn. Off you go.'

She ignored his flat 'no'. 'Dawn is the daughter of Andy, the medical director at our hospital, and his wife Montana,' she told Gianni. 'Montana began the birth centre in Lyrebird Lake and now we have seven midwives and a great team. People drive long distances to give birth here.'

Emma was filling the silence. Not something she usually did. He probably wasn't interested. She kept her eyes on her daughter as she skipped across the grass, but she was tempted to drink in one more close-up appraisal of the drop-dead gorgeous Gianni Bonmarito. Who for some reason she enjoyed teasing. There was something about the snippets told by Angus that captured her imagination. And confirmed the absolute tragedy and darkness she saw in his eyes.

She didn't know why he affected her so deeply, so achingly that she wanted to draw his big swarthy head down on her breast and soothe his brow. Maybe kiss those heavy, lash-framed eyelids and comfort the inner demons she could see in his soul. Grace ran off with Dawn, and Emma turned back to the man beside her and glanced quickly one more time.

New heat that had nothing to do with an unexpectedly warm day tickled her skin. She'd known that final glance would ruin her. She looked away to the house instead. 'I'd better see if I can entice Louisa, Angus's stepmother, out to the group. She should be with us.' And I need to get away from you.

'I will come.' Gianni fell into step beside her and though her brain said, Please don't, she could feel the thrum of awareness between them like a tiny swarm of nuisance gnats that often dusted the lake in the late afternoon. All strange feelings she wasn't usually disturbed with.

She went for lightness. 'So you're good in the kitchen, are you?' It was easier to tease and the thought made her smile. He looked anything but the kind of man who would prepare a meal with his own hands.

'I enjoy cooking. My parents had a wonderful housekeeper who humoured me in the kitchen. Especially my national dishes. I find the sensuality of food delightful.' An unexpectedly wicked light shone in his eyes and as she intercepted the innuendo his words dusted her cheeks with pink. She promised herself she wouldn't be caught alone with Gianni in a kitchen any time soon and dropped the topic like the hot gnocchi it was.

The silence lengthened and she tumbled into speech. 'I tried to get Louisa to join us before,' she said, 'but she seemed happier focussed on the catering rather than being a part of the group in her loss.'

He didn't answer, didn't help the silence with his own attempt to lighten the awareness between them, until even the way they moved in perfect synchronisation towards the wide wooden steps that led onto the porch stretched her nerves. She'd never met anyone like him.

Politely, Gianni paused to allow her to precede him up the steps. He should say something but he could think of nothing except the way he was aware of her every movement and sway of her hips. Heat flowed between them as she slid past his body, and even though they didn't touch his flesh prickled. His eyes were drawn again to the swing of her slim hips. Hips that enticed as easily as his breath eased in and out. It was the sun raising both their temperatures, he told himself sternly.

The house was a large, many-gabled country home with a stained-glass-edged front door that led to a central hallway. It was dim and cool inside, to his relief, and the scent of furniture oil and eucalyptus grounded him.

He glanced into high-ceilinged bedrooms that led off the hallway and the old-fashioned furniture looked warm and welcoming. Like everything in this town.

She must have seen his look. 'The doctor's surgery and clinic rooms are in the back of the house and have a separate entrance,' Emma said. 'Visiting medical and nursing staff can stay here and Louisa caters for them.' Then they came to the back half of the house. 'This is the heart of the home—Louisa's kitchen.'

Louisa, a round dumpling of a woman with soft pillow breasts that many a tiny child had snuggled into, stood at the old stone sink and stared out the window, a dishcloth lying still in her hand against a cup.

She had the look on her face he'd seen too many times in his work, the grief for a loved one passing, Gianni thought with a rush of sympathy. The look he had seen so frequently in Samoa after the tsunami. Grief that stayed with him late in the night and never allowed his own demons to settle.

Emma crossed the room and rested one hand on the cup in case she startled Louisa into dropping it, and the other arm she slid around the little woman's waist.

'You okay?' Emma's voice was melodic, caring and made the twists in his belly ache harder. He watched her hug Louisa softly in sympathy and Louisa turned her lined face so she could rest her head against Emma's shoulder for a moment.

He could almost taste the comfort the older woman gained. Who was this Emma Rose, compassionately maternal to a woman three times her age? He wondered what had happened in this young woman's life to give her such wisdom beyond her years. It was better to think of this than his whimsy for a hug himself.

But the glimpses of Emma's effect on him had been enough to warn him she was far too dangerous for hugging. Dangerous in a way he hadn't been susceptible to for too many years. In ways he didn't want to be susceptible to ever again.

'I'll be fine.' Louisa sighed and Gianni saw the effort she made to smile. 'I'm just thanking the Lord for the last five years, and the twenty years as his friend before that. He was a good man.'

Emma squeezed her shoulder one more time and then stepped away. 'I know it. And he loved you dearly, as we all do. Is there something we can do for you?' Gianni saw her glance back at him and even that brief acknowledgement was enough to make his belly tighten.

But this Emma was a woman from the other side of the world. A side of the world he was leaving tomorrow. He'd need to remember that.

'Bless you both. No.' The Yorkshire accent seemed broader as Louisa jollied herself back into efficiency. 'I'll come out and sit in the shade with you, though, and enjoy the company of Ned's family and friends.'

'Your family and friends,' Emma corrected gently.

'Aye, of course,' she said, and sighed.

Together the three of them moved out to the lawn and Gianni walked on Louisa's other side so that she was drawn into the group under the tree and settled in a comfortable chair.

Gianni watched as she was fussed over and one of the women handed her a baby to nurse. Instantly Louisa was diverted. He looked at Emma who unobtrusively nodded with satisfaction.

He liked it that she was pleased the older woman was comforted. The feel of these people made him think of the best times he'd had as a child. Times he and his brother had escaped to play with the happy-go-lucky village children where such a sense of support and warmth had been unburdened by the responsibility of being part of the most important family. Carefree. Like Emma made him feel. He needed to put distance between them. Even a little would help prevent his fingers from stroking her cheek because he could imagine the silk beneath his fingers too vividly. 'Perhaps you'd like a glass of punch, Emma?' Gianni indicated the cloth-covered table under the tree.

'I'll come with you.' Emma glanced down at

Louisa, who had buried her nose in the baby's hair. 'Louisa is settled.'

'Well done,' he said quietly as they walked away. 'The innocence of children is precious and a comfort even in terrible times.'

'That's true,' Emma said, looking up at him. 'Is that what you see often in your work?'

He had no idea why he would talk of something he never mentioned. He shrugged and ladled a glass of punch, watched her take a sip and found himself talking to distract himself from her mouth. 'I have seen many families suffer great losses but the safe delivery of one child can restart hope and life like nothing else.'

'Angus said you began working with the rescue forces not long after he did.'

'If not for Angus, I wouldn't be here. Did he tell you he pulled me from an earthquake's land-slide? I'd been buried two days and all others had given up.' Did he tell you I had been on a road to wasting my life before that?

She smiled gently, her eyes intent on his face. 'Yes, but very briefly. Did you think he would tell me much?'

Gianni laughed, but without relief. 'No. I suppose not. We do tend not to speak of what we see. And he spoke of his work even less than I do now.'

'Which comes at a cost as tragic memories accumulate,' she said with great insight. She returned to the thing he wished she'd forgotten. 'Two days buried would give a lot of time for thought.'

'Hmm.' A long time to regret things in the past. He'd almost come to peace with those memories but perhaps they were covered under the new ones he'd collected.

She tilted her head and he felt her concentration not as curiosity but like balm to his hurts. 'I like to think good comes of everything. Even something that seems horrible at the time. What good came of that, Gianni?'

He was distracted by the way she said his name. Softly, rolling the vowels as if savouring the strangeness of them. He supposed his name was strange in this place of Jacks and Johns and Joes. But she was waiting and he needed to think of his answer.

Normally he would have ignored such a question, not that it had been asked before, but for this Emma, strangely he found he could answer honestly. 'It was a long time ago but, yes, it changed my life and created a need to do something useful. Like Angus did. I had been given back my life and I would not waste it again.'

She smiled at him. 'Had you been so useless before?'

He thought of the fast cars, the wild and thoughtless men and women he'd peopled his life with after Maria's death, but that was in the past and another tragedy—though one without a good result. 'I fear so.' His voice lowered as the memories returned. Memories he had to banish every time he was confronted with a similar event. 'Lying there, unable to move, barely able to breathe as I listened to those around me grow silent, made me swear that life was too precious to waste.'

He shook away the memories and forced himself to smile at her, 'But enough of me. You say you are a midwife. Have you always wished that? Like your little Grace has told me she has?'

'Some of the best people I know are midwives.' She grinned at him. Daring him to dispute a fact he knew little about. He had not known any midwives well enough to judge but he knew he liked this one.

'Like Montana and Mia and Misty.' She gestured with her hand at the colourful throng of people she worked with at Lyrebird Lake. 'Wise women and wonderful friends,' she went on. 'Like them, I consider my work a privilege.'

He understood that but it was rare for a person to say it. 'As I do mine.' He shrugged. 'So now we can be happy we have worthwhile lives, though I fear I may be a trifle too focussed on the excuse not to lead a more facetted life.' He grimaced in self-mockery. 'And what do you do for yourself, Emma?'

She glanced around for her daughter. 'I am also a mother.'

He smiled down at her perplexed frown. 'A mother, yes, and a good one, I think. And for Emma—the woman?'

She narrowed her eyes at him and declined to answer, preferring to fire it back at him. 'What do you do for the man, Gianni?'

Someone called out to her and she looked away. And then she smiled at him and was gone. He watched her go. Couldn't not watch her. An intriguing and magnetic woman he hadn't expected to meet. But his life would never change.

CHAPTER TWO

Two hours later Emma found herself looking around for Gianni.

He would be gone tomorrow, which was as well because the fascination inside her seemed to revel in every brooding glance he sent her way. There was an escalating excitement in her stomach unlike anything she'd felt before, and as she checked on her daughter, she realised that she missed seeing Gianni in her peripheral vision.

She needed to remember he'd go back to the drama and tension of emergency rescue with the international taskforce that Angus had retired from five years ago and she'd go back to her work.

But her mind wasn't ready to relegate Gianni

to a past experience. And she rearranged the knowledge she had in her brain and teased at it as if she could glean more.

So Angus had dragged the barely conscious Italian from the rubble and inspired him. Well, it had certainly sparked an unlikely friendship between the two men. And there was at least a ten-year gap in their ages.

Where had she been ten years ago when that had happened?

At school certainly. Not a teen mother yet. Her own mother still well and oblivious to the cloud that would destroy her life and cast a shadow over her family. But she wouldn't go there.

When this Italian intruder was gone, Emma would go back to life in Lyrebird Lake as if he'd never been, which was a good thing.

Ah. There he was. She found him talking to Angus and as if he'd felt her gaze he looked up. For a moment their eyes held and then Angus said something else and Gianni looked away.

Hurriedly she walked on and berated herself for being drawn to him. But what could a girl do when she found herself so aware of a man?

Since their first conversation, whenever she'd moved to another group to talk, shortly afterwards he too would arrive to join the circle and always that thrum of awareness rumbled between them. He'd seemed no more than a few steps away from her all afternoon, despite the fact he barely spoke to her. She sifted through everything Angus had told her as she waited for him to come to her again. Strange how she knew he would.

'So you'll be gone tomorrow,' she said without preamble when he appeared to stand beside her.

'That is true.'

A tennis ball from the cricket game rolled to her feet like a faceless yellow bird and she picked it up and tossed it back to the bowler, glad of the distraction while she bolstered up her courage.

'It's a shame you can't stay a while and see more of the area around Lyrebird Lake.'

His glance swept over her. 'If I had known it would be so beautiful here I would not have made plans.' He smiled. 'Would you have shown me around, Emma?'

She could have found a little time. If he was that attracted to the place, why leave so quickly? 'Perhaps. And your plans can't be changed?'

He gestured fatalistically with his hands and she had to smile at the pure Mediterranean gesture. 'I go to see my brother. It is arranged. We haven't spoken in years. It is time.'

More snippets of the man. 'Did you fall out? Is he married?'

'Such questions.' But he smiled as he said it. 'He too has lost his wife now, so the reason for our disagreement is past.' That sounded even more intriguing and just a little tough on the poor wife, but she hesitated to persist.

She was glad she hadn't offended him with her inquisitiveness.

But everything about him spoke of a different culture, a different life experience, and sometimes she despaired of ever experiencing a world away from Lyrebird Lake. She'd begun to think that she'd pinned her lack of experience of the world onto Gianni's multiculturalism and that was what was drawing her to him. It was as good a reason as any.

Maybe it was the fact that he was going that gave her permission to try and peer into that other world. She couldn't ever remember being so fascinated by a man as this Gianni. 'Tell me what it was like, growing up in Italy. Tell me about your parents.'

She suddenly realised how bold that sounded. 'I'm not normally nosy. But you intrigue me.' She frowned at herself and shook her head again. 'Please don't answer if you prefer not to.'

He smiled sardonically and raised his

impossibly black eyebrows. 'And if I don't, will you walk away?'

She almost said maybe, and then corrected herself. She had never been a coquette. Why lie? She smiled. 'Of course not.' He was too compelling.

He shrugged his impossibly broad shoulders as if to say he couldn't imagine why she would be interested but he would humour her. 'Then I will tell you a little. My parents were both doctors but died in a boating accident when I was a teenager. I was held above the water, unconscious, by my brother until help came.'

'That must have been heartbreaking for two teenage boys.'

He nodded. 'If I had not hit my head, perhaps we could have saved them both, but that is all in the past.' The bleakness was back in his eyes and she'd wished she could retract her question about his parents. Not all of those memories were in the past. She resisted the urge to touch his shoulder in sympathy.

But he went on, almost as if he too was aware time was running out for both of them. 'Leon, older by two years than I, runs the Bonmarito Private Hospitals in Rome. In our family it is our custom for the sons to attend medical school and then marry the wife chosen by the family.'

She couldn't imagine being married to a man she barely knew, especially one as blatantly masculine as this man, but bizarrely she had no problem picturing the scenario.

'So you and Leon did that? Yours was an arranged marriage?' When he nodded she shook her head. What must his wife have thought as he'd approached the marriage bed? Or had she been glad he had been young and handsome?

'*Si*. And no prospect of divorce if it didn't work in the beginning.' He watched her shock with a flicker of sardonic amusement. Even at her expense, she was glad to see him lighten his mood a little. 'The statistics for good marriages in my country are similar to yours,' he said.

'And was your marriage a happy one?'

The bleakness swept back into his eyes. 'By the time she died I had fallen in love with my wife. Yes.'

Ouch. Conversation stopper. What was she doing asking such personal questions? And at a funeral? Weren't they all depressed enough?

The last golden rays of the sun began to dust the trees across the lake and it was time for the party to break up. Time for her to say goodbye to this tragically enigmatic Italian and get on with her own life.

'Thank you for your company, Gianni. I've enjoyed talking to you. I hope I haven't annoyed you with my silly questions.' She smiled at him but didn't offer her hand. Pure self-preservation on her part. 'Have a safe trip home.'

She looked across to the activity. 'I must help

clear up. Louisa is going to Angus and Mia's house for tonight.' Emma could see Misty and Montana gathering glasses and plates from benches.

Gianni nodded and inclined his head as he watched her walk away. Such things he'd not spoken of for years. His words escaping from his mouth like suddenly released prisoners. It was a wonder she hadn't run away from him, not walked. He shook his head and glanced around, looking for Angus. Angus waved at the bench he wanted to move and Gianni strode across, glad to have something physical he could do.

They brought the last of the chairs inside as Montana touched Emma's shoulder for attention. He couldn't help but overhear.

'Emma. I know it's a favour, but I wondered if Grace could sleep over with Dawn tonight…' Montana pointed out of the kitchen window to the veranda. 'She's really missing Ned. I think a little friend might help just for tonight.'

Angus had told him Montana had been the first midwife to board in Ned and Louisa's home and Dawn had been a baby then.

He watched Emma glance out the kitchen window at the two earnest young heads together on the swing.

She nodded and he heard her say, 'That's fine. We were having an early night anyway. I'm taking her up to see Mum tomorrow afternoon.' Then he had the next piece of furniture to move and the rest of the conversation was lost.

In her peripheral vision Emma saw Gianni and Angus move outside to search for more chairs and suddenly it was easier to concentrate. Montana nodded her thanks. 'How is your mother?'

Emma thought of waving hands and erratic attempts to walk. 'She didn't seem as sad last week, but her moods swing pretty wildly. I just wish I could keep her at home but she's even too much in the care she's in sometimes. I don't know what I'll do if she has to leave the centre in Brisbane. And Dad misses the lake.'

Montana hugged her. 'There's no easy answer and we'll be here for you if you need to talk.'

'I know.' Emma shook off the melancholy of worry that she worked so hard to hide and returned to the practical. 'What time do you want me to pick up Grace in the morning?'

'It's Saturday. Sleep in. We'll go shopping early and I'll drop her home before lunch, if that's okay.'

Emma nodded as Louisa came back into the kitchen with her overnight bag and suddenly everyone was ready to leave.

Home wasn't far and Emma declined the offer of a lift in Montana's bus-like vehicle. The evening was cool and it would be good to clear her head in the twilight breeze. To have space to mull over the day on the silent walk home.

The sudden loud snap of a breaking twig pierced her reverie and her head flew up. Then she heard the unmistakable scrape of a shoe on gravel behind her just before a tall shadow loomed over her.

Emma's heart flipped like those silver fish did every afternoon in the lake and her hand came up to her throat as if to hold back a squeak. Up until now the idea of being nervous of the encroaching darkness had never crossed her mind. This was Lyrebird Lake and the safest place she knew. But at that moment her heart galloped crazily as she tried to pierce the gloom to see the person's identity.

'Who is looking after you?' Gianni spoke quietly, but there was a tinge of outrage in his voice.

She peered through the dimness and confirmed it was his face. 'Gianni!' Her shoulders dropped as she breathed heavily out in an exasperated sigh. 'Around here we don't sneak up and scare people. As long as no one does what you just did, I don't need looking after.' She sighed again as her pulse rate settled. She tapped her chest as if to reassure her heart all was well. 'You frightened the life out of me.' She started to walk again.

His dark brows almost touched each other. 'You should not be walking alone, it is almost dark. Please let me drive you to your house.'

Emma rolled her eyes. 'I thought accepting lifts from strangers was dangerous?' she said dryly. She glanced around. Now they were standing closer to the streetlamp but between the orange pools of each lamp it was pretty deserted and darker than she'd realised. But until the silly man had put the notion in her head she'd been happy.

'Come,' he said imperiously, and held out his hand.

Emma looked down at his strong brown fingers, even darker in the dim light, and considered the implications of his touch. Did she want to feel the warmth that she just knew was going to stay with her? She didn't think so.

Emma avoided his hand and turned to his car. 'All right.' But as she reached for the door handle his fingers were there before her.

'May I?' he said. 'Please allow me?'

Emma stood back as he glided the door open. Touchy Italian, she thought. 'No problem. Feel free. I'm just out of practice with people opening doors for me.' She swung herself into the low-slung seat and glanced around the interior of the European sports car.

She read the label of the owner's manual on the console. She'd never been in a Maserati before. Her door clicked shut beside her shoulder and she forced herself to relax back into the seat. The leather was doeskin soft and she wiggled her shoulders in it. Nice. Different from what she was used to, that was for sure.

When he climbed in and secured his seat belt she leaned forward slightly, anticipating the car's forward movement. When it didn't happen she frowned and resisted drumming her fingers. He continued to linger and she turned to look at him with narrowed eyes. And you're waiting for…? she thought with rising suspicion.

'Would you like me to fasten your belt for you?' He'd turned to face her and she realised she'd forgotten the obvious. She bit her lip. The man was scrambling her brains the way her hands were scrambling to get the clasp done up before, heaven forbid, he did help her.

'Does the roof go up?' She was gabbling but suddenly it was very close inside the car.

'No.' He reached forward and the engine started with a muted roar. 'It's a coupé. A Cambiocorsa 2007. I have one at home.'

'Really? Only one?' she said straight-faced. The car was black and low to the ground. She could see that. But she doubted she'd ever feel the need to hire one. 'So you drove down from Brisbane? This is a hire car?' And he had one at home. He was certainly from a different world.

His profile shifted as he glanced at her. 'Are you interested in cars?'

Was she? The subject wasn't one she'd buy a magazine on. 'Not really.'

He nodded as if the answer was what he expected. 'Then let us not discuss them.' End of discussion.

Emma blinked. He'd assumed a protective and almost fatherly role, and Emma wasn't sure she liked it. Well, she was no doormat for obedience. Think of your own topic, then, buddy, she thought. He didn't offer any other conversational gambit and the silence stretched.

He was going tomorrow, she told herself, which made it acceptable if she gave in. 'I live straight down this road. Barely worth driving, in fact,' she said with less than subtle pointedness.

'*Si*. And I also do not live far from here as I have rented a chalet at the Lakeside.' He glanced across and then away. 'They have a fine restaurant. Italian.' She could hear the smile in his voice, and she wondered if it was just because it was almost dark and she had to rely on other senses or if it was because for the first time today he'd smiled broadly enough that it affected his voice. She was glad she couldn't see the curve of his lips. She'd been trying not to look at the sinful promise of his mouth all day. No doubt the sight would haunt her.

'So?' he said.

What on earth was he saying? 'So, what?'

He sighed. Patiently, as if with a child, and with this man she was beginning to feel like one. Not something she'd felt since she the age of sixteen and not something she decided she enjoyed. 'Will you join me for a meal, please, Emma?'

Her heart did that fish thing again. Now? 'Aren't you going back to Angus's?'

He shook his head once in the dimness. 'His

stepmother is there tonight. I dined with him last night and we talked. I will lunch with him tomorrow before I leave.'

Emma filled the silence while she considered the implications of his invitation. 'Angus had a wonderful relationship with Ned since he'd made up with his father.' Her mind skittered to the idea of dining alone with Gianni in an intimate setting and away again. Her thoughts went back to Angus. It was safer. 'He seems to be at peace with Ned's passing.'

'Yes.' Gianni inclined his head while he contemplated her profile. 'Thankfully they had time to enjoy each other's company. And Angus was instrumental in my recent contact with my brother. But you haven't answered my question.'

The guy had a single focus. She went with the answer she'd known she'd make from the beginning. To live dangerously. 'Perhaps. I need to eat.' She looked down at her grubby skirt that she'd played cricket in. 'I'd like to get changed, though.'

He nodded again. 'How much time do you need?'

She thought about it. How much did she really need? Five minutes. 'Half an hour,' she said.

'Good.' Satisfaction was obvious. 'Much faster than I expected.'

She tried vainly not to smile and she hoped he didn't see or think she was making fun of him. 'It's this house, with the roses over the gate.'

She lifted her hand to the handle and his fingers came over the top to stay it. 'Please wait for me to open it,' he said quietly, and her hand froze under his. She sighed and leaned back against the leather.

She'd been right. His skin was warm and made the gooseflesh pop up on her arms like bubbles in the muddy sand at the edge of the lake. His hand moved away and she would have sworn his fingers were still there. Hot over hers.

If he could do that with just a touch, she was in big trouble if she invited anything else. But she wouldn't. It was just a meal, she was feeling flat after the funeral and Grace was away, and she didn't get to eat at the Lakeside very often. Never had, actually.

He opened her car door and she climbed out. It seemed a waste of energy to her but the cosseting was strangely compelling. He ushered her through the gate and up the path to her front door like an old-fashioned footman. Then waited while she unlocked the door and only left her when she entered her house, but he didn't drive away until she'd shut the door.

She heard the roar of the car as it accelerated away and Emma's heart flopped around as she leant back against the closed door. Her hand actually slid to her throat where her pulse pounded. What had happened to her in the last five minutes? It had just been a lift a few hundred metres but she felt vibrantly alive. Ridiculously so.

There were a hundred good reasons not to be attracted to this man, or any man for that matter, and fifteen good reasons to wallow in it.

The hundred were all complications and she didn't need them.

The fifteen were about the number of good years she estimated she had before the disease that had turned her graceful and gracious mother into a tormented bed-ridden shell of a woman could begin to do the same to her.

Fifty per cent chance of having the gene. In the last few years Emma had toyed briefly with the idea of taking the final genetic test, a test that could prove her fate irrevocably, but she'd always come back to that tiny spark of hope she'd not inherited the predisposing gene. She didn't think she'd cope if that hope was gone. She couldn't give up that tiny beam of optimism that once lost would never return.

Her arms crept around her waist and Gianni was forgotten, everything was forgotten, as her worst nightmare touched her again with cold fingers of dread.

The fear was for Grace, her daughter, and the fact that if Emma was shadowed then Grace had a fifty per cent chance of having it, too. Emma couldn't do it. At this time in her life she couldn't live with Grace being positive for Huntington's disease.

Instead, Emma lived her life as if she had only until she turned forty, like her mother had before she'd become ill, and she saved every penny to ensure Grace would have the choices for the support Emma might not be able to give.

But for this moment Emma was alive, she was well, and apparently she was an attractive woman. Not something she'd thought about for a very long time. She didn't know when she'd decided that she *wanted* to savour a little of what Gianni had to offer. If he was offering anything apart from a meal, that was.

She'd never looked for another boyfriend after

she and Tommy had drifted apart. She'd been too busy. Too focussed.

As two sixteen-year-olds she and Tommy had discovered they'd little in common except Grace, and Emma had been sensible enough not to tie herself to a man she'd already grown out of. Tommy had left to see the world with Emma's blessing. But maybe she'd missed out on the subtle thrill of a man's appreciation.

In fact, even with the little exposure to Gianni's attention today she'd begun to revel in the unfamiliar feeling of being a fragile flower to be cherished and taken care of. Not something she had any experience of and no doubt it would irk her very quickly in the real world, but this was an out-of-the-ordinary opportunity to let herself be spoiled.

And there was something about Gianni that called to her in a way she'd never heard before. Heaven forbid, there might be a fabulous encounter her body was trying to tempt her into, and the idea had a compulsive magnetism, like the man did. As long as she was careful and it didn't get out of hand.

Gianni was right out of her comfort zone. And he was leaving soon. To go back to Italy. If she made a fool of herself, he was a ship in the night with a home port she couldn't get much further away from than inland Queensland.

She looked at her watch and bounced away from the door as if someone had poked her with a cattle prod. She'd wasted five minutes!

CHAPTER THREE

TWENTY-FIVE minutes later Gianni knocked on Emma's door and the sound echoed through Emma's chest and under her ribcage. Boom. Boom. Boom. He was here. She couldn't remember the last time she'd had a real date. Probably never.

She sucked in her breath and ran her tongue inside her gums to make sure she didn't have any lipstick on her teeth. Still not convinced, she grimaced toothily at the mirror on the way to her door. Yep. All was well. Another deep breath as she paused and hoped she'd dressed right. She opened the door.

Christo. Gianni sucked his own lungful of air. Emma's blonde hair was loose over her shoulders and she'd abandoned the pink lipstick for a deep sultry red that matched the lush material of her blouse. To call it a blouse was a blasphemy. The soft material clung like a skin and lingered like his eyes on the swell of her breasts and plunged, also like his eyes, down into a V of paradise.

His breath jammed for a moment and then resumed, like his mesmerised surveillance of her preparations. All this in half an hour?

He'd never been attracted to trousers on women, preferring the femininity of a swirling skirt, but when she twirled to show him, the way her firm buttocks snuggled into the stretchy black material made his eyes blink. Then she moved back further to open the door for him and he could see it hung almost like a skirt, lots of fabric swirling around her legs from the tight tapering waist, teasing him with the thought of it in a pool of darkness at her feet.

'Hello?' Her voice broke the spell and he blinked and swore again in his head. What was it about this woman that grabbed him by the throat and demolished his brain?

'*Bella.* You are beautiful and took my breath away.'

She laughed. Softly, and to him like the musical bells of his favourite chapel. Everything she did entranced him. 'Thank you.' she said. 'The men around here would be far too embarrassed to say that out loud.'

He frowned. 'I speak the truth.' He glanced around the inside of her house. A welcoming room, evidence of a family and very clean. But he wanted her in the dark, beside him in the close confines of the car, somewhere he could inhale her scent and absorb the vibrations her body caused in his. With no distractions. 'Shall we go?'

'Did you manage to get a table in the restaurant?'

He frowned again. Why would he not? 'Of course.' She glanced away and shook her head slightly, and he was teased by the tiny smile she tried to hide. 'I amuse you?'

'Very much so. But it's nice because you are so very different from the men around here.' She walked past him onto the veranda, the hint of roses she left in her wake teasing him almost more than her words, and then she handed him her house keys. 'I'm guessing you want to lock the door?'

'*Grazie*. You learn.' Her profile against the lights from the veranda made his eyes gleam. Did she have no idea how seductive she looked in those trousers? He had changed his preferences already.

'I'm a smart woman.' She tossed her head teasingly.

The movement exposed her throat to the light. 'And very beautiful.'

'I could get used to this.' He heard the whispered words but was sure he'd not been meant to. How could this woman not have a hundred men beating a path to her door? It was a tragedy he went home tomorrow or he would have shown her what she deserved—or maybe it was a good thing. Either way he could introduce her to the way she should be cared for tonight.

As Gianni followed her down the path and under the rose arch he had the sudden urge to reach out and halt her progress, turn her beautiful face toward him and taste the promise he saw while the heady fragrance drifted around them, but he held back. Something he would regret later. No doubt the scent of roses would remind him of this moment that could have been.

This time she'd waited beside the car for him to open the door and the sleeping animal inside him growled complacently at securing her compliance. That beast had been dormant for a very long time and he'd forgotten the taste of cosseting a woman.

When she was seated he bent to lift a swathe of material from the hem of her trousers that had fallen outside the door and the material cascaded across his palm and fell like liquid around her tiny feet. All sensory input that teased him more. He clenched his fingers as he moved back to shut the door before he trod with restrained haste to join her. Still he could feel the material, cool and seductive like the woman who awaited him. She had him entranced.

Gianni's door closed quietly as he was seated and Emma felt the car shrink to only the space between them. Yet not claustrophobic. Different. It felt intimate and exciting, and every nerve in her body seemed to be waving its receptors at the man beside her. Strange feelings for a woman who thrived on control and organisation.

He glanced across before he started the engine and it was as if he touched her. A slow caress. Hurriedly she did up her seat belt.

He smiled, and his eyes seemed to glow like a brown-eyed tiger, and her belly kicked. 'I could have helped,' he said.

She rubbed her arms. Not likely, buddy. The thought of his hand at her waist gave her more goose-bumps.

'Do you live in your house all alone?'

She raised her eyebrows at him but doubted he'd see that in the dashboard light. 'Not something I should tell a man I barely know.'

'Good,' he said, and she laughed again. He was funny. And old-fashioned, and yet she had the feeling that his moral code might bend dramatically when it was his own desires that were at stake. She didn't think he realized how at sea she was. Luckily.

She looked out the window and back again. 'I live with my daughter. My father comes sometimes to stay when he can and my brothers used to live there but the last of them has just married. They're all shift workers so they used to come and go a lot anyway.'

'In my country, alone in a house is not good

for a woman and her daughter. It is different here?'

She frowned. Now he'd annoyed her. Though, if she was honest, maybe a little of her response was due to the fact she didn't want to think about the example she was setting to her daughter by going out with a man who made her feel sexy for the first time in her life. 'Yes,' she said shortly. 'My daughter is safe. Lyrebird Lake is a safe place. We have very little crime. I know everyone in town.'

His heavy brows drew together. 'And people don't drift through?' His voice was dry. 'I'm sure Angus said there is a working mine? A transient miner population only up the road.'

She tilted her head at him. Defiantly. 'Where I live is fine. And not your concern.' His interest had become too pointed. 'In this country customs differ. Did you say we would eat?'

He sat back, and then nodded. 'My apologies. It is none of my business.' He started the car and of course now she felt guilty… But then she shrugged in the dark. He could get over it. Get used to the way women could look after themselves in Australia. Had to look after themselves. She thought with amusement about Tommy and her brothers, and the way she more looked after them. They should fly a women's independence flag for her at Lyrebird Lake.

No conversation occurred until they drove into the cobbled courtyard of the Lakeside and the restaurant lights spilled into the car park and reflected back off the water.

She stayed in her seat, very tempted to open her own door just to tease him, but that would be petty. Was she bored with his old-fashioned manners already? Her door swung away and he held his hand out to help her.

'May I assist you?' His voice was low and courteous, no hint of assertiveness as it curled around her like a tender scarf. It was interesting he hadn't presumed this time.

No, she wasn't bored with being spoilt, she thought as she shivered in the sensations and hugged them to herself. His fingers were warm and strong when she took his hand, just like last time, and she felt the same burning sensation up her arm and the tightening of her breasts.

'Are you cold?'

He was genuinely attentive. She didn't know how to deal with the unfamiliarity of his concern. 'A little,' she prevaricated, more to hide her embarrassment, and instantly he slipped his jacket off and the warmth of man-heated silk caressed her shoulders.

Like an unexpected gift the subtle wash of his aftershave mixed with the scent of male bombarded already overloaded senses and her heel slipped on the cobbles under her feet as she actually felt faint for a second.

His arm came around her. 'Are you well?' He frowned down at her. 'It has been an emotional day. Perhaps I should take you home.'

'No, I'm fine. Really.' She straightened out of his embrace and stepped back. 'I just slipped in my heels.' Her heart was thumping in her chest like a drum and she took a long cool breath of the night air into her lungs and stood tall. Or as tall as she could with her height. Despite the pinching in her toes she definitely needed high heels with this guy. 'I'm fine,' she said again. 'Just a silly slip. Let's go in.'

His brows remained creased, but he nodded reluctantly. 'As you wish.' He glanced over her attire again with a tiny glint in his eyes. 'It would be a shame not to share your beautiful preparations with the world.'

Yes, she thought dryly. She could hardly wait for the gossip. It would fly.

The restaurant was dimly lit with red lamps in brackets on the wall and candles on the tables. Maybe no one would see her. They were led to a white linen-covered table that faced out over the lake, a shiny-green-leafed ficus provided privacy from the next couple and the room buzzed with the hum of quiet conversations.

'And a good table, as well,' Emma said with a glance around, and strangely, for a town she'd grown up in, there wasn't a familiar face to be seen. But other tables seemed as private or strategically placed as theirs so maybe there were. Either way, the town would hear tomorrow that Emma had been out with a *man*! And a stranger.

She handed him back his jacket and Gianni lifted one imperious eyebrow as he waited for her to be seated but didn't comment. She didn't need it when she'd only been covering her nervousness anyway.

She sat and he did too and suddenly her brain froze as she had a brief moment of panic about what conversation she could make with this Italian she barely knew in such an intimate setting. How would they fill the time between courses?

It wasn't like she did this every night. Or spoke to strange men. The only men she conversed with were her family and friends and husbands and partners of women she cared for in labour. Then again, Gianni looked to be socially practised enough for both of them. She hoped.

His pale grey suit shone discreetly and she guessed some designer's label would be sewn inside on silk, and his shirt and tie, though understated, shrieked unlimited funds.

The maître d' draped the starched napkin across her lap and reverently handed her the menu. The choices had no prices, not to trouble her pretty head over cost, she guessed, and she smiled. Well, well, Lyrebird Lake. You multilayered lady. Her country town had city chic. She'd had no idea. Another first, and she was going to enjoy the experience. If it killed her.

Her escort bent his head to discuss wine with the waiter and her eyes were drawn to the harsh lines of Gianni's face. Such a strong and arrogant jaw, angular cheek bones and a Roman nose that proclaimed lineage and power. He could almost be classified as too grand to relax with yet she didn't feel intimidated by him. Especially now she'd decided this was going to be fun.

She wondered why she still felt secure. He was certainly imposing, and so different from any man she knew, but something in his eyes, and perhaps that obscure vulnerability only she seemed to see in the chiselled fullness of his mouth, drew her like a moth to a flame and dared her to touch the light. Thrilled her with danger that crackled along her nerves and dusted the smile on her lips that she couldn't seem to lose.

He took his eyes from the waiter as if he felt her appraisal. His eyebrows lifted and she was trapped. Trapped by his interest, his fascination for her. Trapped by heat. Trapped by the feeling she had to take this moment or regret it for ever. Her brain suggested she look away but there was no way she actually could and her smile dimmed.

The hum from the other diners faded and slowly warmth infused into her skin.

'Champagne?' There was a low caressing nuance in his voice that raised the gooseflesh in a response she couldn't hide.

Emma swallowed, had to to make her voice work. 'Thank you.' What havoc would alcohol wreak on her already shaky control? she mocked herself. Then again, maybe she'd be less agitated.

He indicated with his eyes to the menu, frozen in her hands.

'Have you chosen?'

Food. She'd forgotten food. She flicked a glance at the blur of words on the page. 'It all looks wonderful.'

He smiled. 'Perhaps the seafood platter? For two?'

His knee grazed hers under the table and her

heart skidded like a stone across the water outside. It was ridiculous, the impact of a slide of material on material, but there was no doubt she was as receptive to him as a ripple on the lake.

'Fine,' she managed, and recited *Fun* over and over to herself in her mind as she took a sip of mineral water the waiter had poured. The liquid was cold and delicious and much better for her state of mind than the flute of sparkling wine that arrived magically, complete with moisture-blushed strawberries on a tiny silver salver.

He removed his attention for a moment while he discussed the menu with the waiter and her shoulders sagged a little in relief. When had it stopped being fun and become a battle to prevent her body from leaning towards him so she could sit and stare at him like a gawky teen? She focussed on the reflection of the candlelight on her cutlery.

Cool down. He's just a guy. And you're a professional woman with an eight-year-old daughter.

'So tell me.' His voice made her jump and her gaze flew to his. 'Do you ever leave this town?'

'Every week.' She looked away from him, actually thankful he'd picked a topic that grounded her like no other. 'I visit my mother in Brisbane.' And attend the monthly Huntington's disease meetings and any speaking engagements they'd booked for her to help the cause raise money for research. But she didn't want to go into her personal nightmare.

'So your Grace is used to car travel?'

Where was this leading? 'Grace? Sometimes. Tomorrow she will. She stays with her paternal grandmother every second weekend. They're very close.'

He frowned and she guessed it was confusing. 'And are you close to your daughter's father?'

What had Tommy got to do with it? He was quite happy playing in a band in Holland. 'I'd prefer not to talk about my daughter or her father.'

He didn't answer and she watched his impassive face for a clue. When he spoke it was on a different subject, which was good. He wasn't slow at picking up taboos. 'It has been an interesting visit to your town. The funeral less tragic than I expected. It is a shame I did not plan to stay longer.'

Emma was thinking it was lucky. 'So tell me more about your work,' Emma said.

'I'd prefer not to talk about my work,' he said, and smiled at his mimicry of her. 'But I will tell you that I have been given leave after my last assignment.' He raised his eyebrows at taboo subjects. 'Perhaps it is different for you. Do you wish to talk about your job?'

'I'm always happy to talk about midwifery.' And she did, with flashing eyes, warm reminiscent smiles and anecdotes, the passion and the wonder she saw in a woman giving birth in her voice.

Gianni watched her like a hawk. He'd thought it would be pleasant to bring this woman to dine with him.

Pleasant hadn't happened. Nothing so mediocre.

Her company intrigued him, fascinated him and irritated him with all he didn't understand, and the desire to reach across and bring her wrist to his mouth made his hands clench on the table cloth.

But this wasn't the time or the place for slaking hungers that had suddenly caught up with him. He'd be well to eat quickly and return this woman to her home before it became dangerous for them both. Unfortunately, her enthusiasm had passed from discussing her work, which he regretted, because with the passion she displayed she became even more captivating.

'What of you?' she said. 'Who's at home for you?'

Nobody. 'I have not thought of home for a long time.' He shrugged. 'Haven't for many years. But that may change when I see Leon and settle what is between us. My life will have more direction again perhaps.'

'Nieces and nephews?'

'I have one nephew. He must be eight. My late sister-in-law said I was pompous with children. I've met him once.'

Well, that stopped the conversation. Or did it? She had the feeling he used shock to silence questions. There would be no more chances after tonight to discover what made this man different. What drew her to him? How did she find such a thing out? Questions? She had nothing to lose. 'How long ago did your wife die, Gianni?'

'Ten years.' Bluntly.

She'd been expecting a much more recent loss. There had to be other reasons as well that he hadn't looked for a stable relationship. 'And you've loved her that whole time.'

He raised his eyebrows. The tiger's glint was back and the impact of that flash purred along her arms and she had to stop her hands rubbing the flicker.

'Do you really want to know that?' His voice was deep and low and the awareness of the game she was playing grew with his words. Did she dare to go on?

She did feel reckless. Emboldened by the fact that tonight she could risk learning things other women seemed to know about being a woman. Things she'd never had time for. Or the opportunity. He would leave tomorrow. She'd take him on. 'I'd like to know why I can feel your pain as more recent. Especially if you'd only met your wife just prior to your wedding.'

He inclined his head at her perception. 'You do not hold back, Emma.'

Not tonight. 'Should I?'

He shrugged. 'You are different from the women I've known. They are my own demons. My wife may have died years ago, and it is true we barely knew each other in the month that we had, but it was enough.'

Her voice softened and there was no chance of the question carrying to other tables. 'How did she die, Gianni?'

'Maria wished to see Africa. I thought it a good way to overcome the awkwardness of barely knowing each other.' He grimaced with distaste. 'Since I had been told she loved another on the morning of our wedding.'

Nice well-wisher. Emma felt indignant on his and his poor wife's behalf. 'By…?'

He smiled at her. Aware of her attempt to free him from the ghosts of his past. 'I will humour you for so long…' He left the end of the sentence dangling, like she had. Showing her it was his choice to continue but he would also stop when he decided. She had to be content with that. In truth, he'd offered more than she thought he would. She waited patiently.

'My brother's wife. Whom I suspect enjoyed her moment of triumph, but I must not speak ill of the dead.'

'Why not?' Emma raised her brows and he smiled again and then sobered.

Gianni drew a breath and it was as if he could feel the heat and lush scents of the red earth in Africa all those years ago. He could feel the warm weight of Maria in his arms as he'd sunk to the ground. 'You asked how she died?' He looked at the woman opposite him but she was barely an outline as he remembered.

'On the last day of a safari, a snake, a black mamba, fell from a tree and attacked many times as they both panicked. I had stopped to take a photo and Maria had gone on ahead with one guide.' He remembered her whispers as she clutched at him. And the moment she'd rasped,

'The child I carry isn't yours.' Just when he'd fallen in love.

'It was a long time ago,' Emma's voice was gentle and recalled him to the present. He could hear in her voice the things unsaid that others had repeated over the years. It wasn't his fault. There was nothing he could do. But it had been his duty to protect her.

Just as they'd said when he had survived and his parents had died. But it didn't take away the guilt. These were his crosses to bear. And he made up for it as he could.

'Other women just as precious die every day and so for me my wound can never heal.'

Emma thought about that and risked a guess at what he meant. 'Those you've lost in your work?'

'There are many I cannot save. I do not expect to love again and accept my heart is dry and barren with each new loss.'

His word choice had formalised and she

realised that his honesty had affected him more than he showed. The answer to the price he paid seemed obvious to her. 'Don't you think you've given enough? Perhaps change your area of medicine?'

He shrugged. 'I'm good at it. Will I sit at home and wonder who will save those in need, then?'

One day the price would prove too high. Maybe that time was here. 'Perhaps you should leave the next generation to save the world. Move on, like Angus did.'

He smiled at her, like she was a child, and it annoyed her. Inflamed her actually that he could be so cavalier with the man inside him she wanted to help. 'So easy,' he said.

Her anger dissipated. He was right. Who was she to imagine she understood his dilemma or his pain? But the depth of her need to help him came from a source she had no control over.

Their meal arrived but the topic had sobered them both.

She had no reason to believe she could help this man, didn't know why she wanted to so badly, but when her hand lifted to lie over his she felt his tremor of awareness, felt his heat seep into her, and then his palm turned and she in turn was captured by him.

He leaned forward and drew her fingers towards his mouth and kissed not her hand but the sensitive skin on the inside of her wrist. A salute that sent tiny erotic messages that fluttered her belly before she'd even tasted a mouthful.

'Let us eat,' he said quietly, 'and the night will take care of itself.'

Time and the food blurred, his eyes on her eyes, or on her mouth or on her fingertips, and instead of feeling awkward she felt caressed and savoured and sultry in ways she'd never imagined she could feel, and the conversation between them was more subliminal than spoken.

Two people who should never have met, drawn by fate and tossed by emotions they recognised in each other.

Time slowed. A sip of wine became an invitation for him to watch the curve of her throat, a bite of fish meant a thought of other nips not related to food as they created an aura of sensuality around them like a bubble only they were privy to.

He ordered dessert, a blush-coloured gelato that matched her cheeks and cooled her mouth with a tang that cleaned her palate and made her lips tingle.

'Would you mind if we had our coffee delivered to my chalet? The view over the lake will be worth the walk.'

It wasn't the view she was thinking of when he stood behind her chair and waited. When she rose, his hand rested possessively in the small of her back, barely there yet burning like a brand as he ushered her out of the restaurant to the raised wooden path that ran along the water. Never had she felt so cherished, so feminine, so receptive to another person. Or so at risk of making a mistake.

Just this night, she whispered to herself, two people with tragedy, he in the past and she in the future. Why should she not go with this feeling that swept her into uncharted waters with a man she barely knew but felt she knew more than anyone? For something, a secret part of her pleaded, just for her, Emma. In case she never felt how she felt now ever again. And perhaps she would be able to erase the pain from him, for a while at least, and he from her.

Beside the path they drifted hand in hand. Under a stand of ghostly gums a huge set of silver wind chimes reflected the moonlight and a sultry breeze brushed against them so they spoke to her. They were two people colliding in a world like the pipes of the chimes, his thumb caressing her palm, promising a song that could soar as high as she wished.

As they passed the chimes rattled, first in a whisper as they were puffed by a tendril of wind and then in a cathedral refrain as the increasing breeze stirred them to greater excitement—like the way her heart beat gathered speed and intensity within her chest as she walked the path with Gianni.

They came to a chalet that stood a little distance away, larger than the others, right down on the edge so that the actual supports for the building stood over the water and the steps ran up the side and around the building like a decoration on a cake.

His hand lifted from her back, still touching but with no pressure, to guide her up the stairs in case she suffered second thoughts. She missed the heat and the connection and arched back so that he leant on her again.

'Just checking,' he whispered into her neck as

he followed her up the stairs, and the warmth of his breath blushed her skin with a need she could barely contain. Where had these feelings come from and how could something so dangerous dwell inside sensible her? She had no idea but she didn't wish them away.

'You promised coffee,' she murmured, 'and a moonlight view I'd be impressed with.'

'I will offer you that and any more you wish, my little temptress, and the view I too am waiting to see.'

She stepped onto the little deck and leant her hands on the rail to gaze out over the moonlit lake, with him directly behind her. His chest against her shoulders, hot and heavy, his hips pressed against her back and with an unmistakable bulge of hardness against her spine. His thighs against her buttocks.

Solid masculine heat against her, and she pushed herself back into his body because she could not stop the urge to do so. They fused from shoulder to thigh and she'd never felt anything so glorious as they both stood under the starlit sky. In the distance she could still hear the chimes as the breeze rose and fell.

He stepped away and she frowned in confusion but then saw that the coffee had arrived. Gianni pulled out her chair and she sat, externally demure, as the cups were laid and the tall silver coffee pot set on the table with a small basket of chocolates.

'Grazie,' Gianni said.

'Great spot for it,' the waiter said, nodded at the water and left.

Great spot for what? Emma thought, and smiled to herself like the cat with the cream. She had no idea where her scruples had gone, departed without notice, and she didn't want them back just yet. She slipped her shoes off, and they fell with tiny clunks to the floor, and when she put her bare foot down Gianni had placed his foot under hers so that her sole rested on his ankle.

Gianni could not take his eyes of this vision in the moonlight. The fine bones of her cheeks shadowed the flawless skin beneath and the tilt of her mouth curved up at him like the moon itself, promised such delights that made him want to take her face in his hands and worship her.

Then her bare toes touched his leg and the shaft of desire speared through him like an arrow straight to his heart.

'Well, hello,' he said. 'It seems there is an intruder under the table.' Her foot stilled and he leaned across and took her wrist again to draw it to his mouth. 'Do not stop, for I have just discovered a fetish with feet I did not know I had.' He smiled at her and slipped his shoe off and their feet writhed around each other in a heated duel that was ridiculously erotic.

'I'm not a practised flirt,' she said, and would have hung her head if he hadn't slipped one finger under her chin to lift her face to the light.

'I think you will manage. Practice is not something you need.' He shook his head. 'Do you have any idea how beautiful you look? How I am still unable to believe I have this moonlit angel in my lair?'

She shook her head and her silvered hair shimmered in the night. 'Perhaps I'm no angel,' she said, and he smiled.

'I hope not.'

'And this is just one night.' There was resolution in her voice he couldn't miss. 'For mutual comfort in a cruel world.' Did she need to clarify?

He understood. A night for a future they would not share. For the past she would like him to finally lay to rest. For all those he couldn't save and never would. For something in her that needed comfort. He wanted to draw her down onto his chest and protest against fate. He wanted to tell her that this night was only a beginning but he could see she didn't want to hear that.

He rose and drew her up into his arms. Carried her into the dimly lit chalet that waited for them where he offered her his heart to hide in.

CHAPTER FOUR

WHEN Emma woke in the morning, after many desultory and delicious awakenings in the night, she could see the pinking of the lake as the morning sun threatened to rise in the east and felt the glow in the heat of her ears.

How was she ever going to emotionally move on from last night? Her muscles ached. Then again, how was she going to physically move? She couldn't help the tiny smile that curved her lips. That sinfully erotic tango they'd danced in the cabin had been the start but certainly not the end of her dance lessons.

Then reality crashed in. It was morning and today he left the country.

Her hand was captured in his and as she turned

she found Gianni's eyes on her. He lifted her fingers to his mouth and kissed them one by one, and her eyes stung as she held back the tears of loss.

Why couldn't he have been asleep? Made it easy. Or at least easier. She needed to get out of here before she threw herself on his chest and begged him not to go. Begged him to take her back to the place they'd discovered last night and this morning that excluded the world and all its tragedies, and left only them, fingers still entwined, joined against fate.

'Good morning, my angel.'

She swallowed the prickles in her throat. 'Good morning.' She sat up and her hand fell from his as she clutched the sheet to her naked breast. Why hadn't she slipped away in the night and avoided this awkwardness? Why didn't he get up and leave her to slink away.

His black brows creased and he stroked her cheek with one finger. 'I will not have you think the thoughts that chase across your beautiful face. What we have shared could never be wrong, or embarrassing, or regretted.'

Easy for him. She was a mother. 'Maybe not on your side.' But she was also a woman, a tiny voice inside cried out.

'There is no shame in such a gift and I will not have you tarnish it with such thoughts.' He tilted her chin. 'Thank you, Emma. For sharing your soul with me in a night I will never forget.'

She could see he meant it and gradually the awkwardness fell away, to be replaced by a tiny flicker of pride at the awe in his face—awe that she'd put there. Maybe it had been what she'd intended. And if she could just get home before the world awoke, she could hug the night to herself and allow the memories the place they deserved and dream that she had touched him and maybe healed him a little.

'Thank you, Gianni. You're right.' She leaned across and kissed him, once on the lips and then on the cheek. 'I'll shower and then I'd like to go before the sun comes up.'

'Si.'

Gianni watched her rise and the gentle light stroked her pale thighs like his hand ached to do as she walked away. But distance was between them now, she'd put it there, and he couldn't blame her. She'd been so generous, too generous, and he didn't know how he would be able to go on without having her in his arms, wrapping her close to his body until they were one because what he'd found there had touched the core of him… But he'd promised. No future, no past, no hope for anything more than the memories of a night he would never forget. The sooner he left this place the better.

Fifteen minutes later, as they slipped around the sleeping buildings to his car, the sweet carol of the chimes drifted towards them and they looked at each other and smiled. Yet as they passed the gumtree stand no hint of breeze stirred in the air and the metal tubes hung frozen in the early morning light. Emma's forehead puckered.

Strange, she thought, until from a darker patch of greenery a rustle and a crackle in the undergrowth heralded the arrival of a small brown bird, his lyre tail spread and stately as he poked his beak at them.

They stopped, arrested by the sight of nature so fearlessly regarding them, then enthralled as suddenly the male lyrebird shared his song again—the perfect mimic of the cathedral chimes—pure and true as if a magical wind danced the noise from the pipes that hung soundlessly from the branch above him.

Emma's hand tightened in Gianni's as they stood, and the pressure was returned as spellbound below the silent hanging chimes they waited for the song to finish. A tranquil peace stole over her and dissipated any remains of awkwardness that had hung between them. Their eyes met.

Emma felt gooseflesh cover her arms. 'It's a lyrebird,' she whispered. 'I've seen one sing only once before and that was on the day my Grace was born,' Emma said. And suddenly she knew that what she and Gianni had shared could never be wrong. As if satisfied, the bird turned and disappeared into the bush. Quietly they walked on.

The lyrebird's song kept Emma calm all through the morning as she prepared to travel to Brisbane to see her mother. She filled her time until Grace returned and desperately tried to block out the need to know if Gianni had left while she searched for tasks to divert herself.

Once, a sudden thought drove all hard-won peace from her mind, and asked pedantically if she was perfectly sure she wouldn't suffer any other complications from the night.

Her hand stilled as she considered again the possibility she'd dismissed. No. They'd been careful. He'd been assiduous even, and she couldn't be that fertile twice.

The night was gone, her choice had been made, and now she needed to concentrate on the real world.

In the following weeks, in snippets, she learnt that Gianni had been in contact with Angus, and that Gianni and his brother had reconciled. At a netball game she overheard that Gianni had again contacted Angus, and Emma tried not to listen.

For Gianni it was as if his life had restarted with Lyrebird Lake. It hadn't just been the delectable Emma, it had been the friendship of Angus and his friends and the warmth of the whole town. His visit had coloured his grey world and now he and Leon had recaptured a little of the rapport of their youth. It seemed his brother's marriage had been less than perfect, too.

When Angus had rung to ask a favour, Gianni had agreed without hesitation before being tied to the opening of the new Bonmarito Private

Hospital in Venice at the end of the year. Gianni had realised it was time to change not just his job but his life. A life that could be become more rounded to include others.

A month later Gianni parked his rented Maserati outside the old doctor's residence and switched off the engine.

He hoped this temporary move to Lyrebird Lake was the right thing to do. On the surface it had been Angus's idea, to cover while the more senior man had been roped into a diplomatic mission in Vienna for a month, leaving a temporary vacancy at the hospital.

Gianni had planned to stay at the Lakeside, memories of his night with Emma a powerful inducement, but Angus had pushed for him to stay at the old doctor's residence as company for Louisa. So here he was.

Gianni knew all about crushing grief when one lost their partner in life. He'd seen it so many times in his work.

Then, very quickly after his arrival, early tomorrow he would start at the hospital.

It was impossible for him to stop the irresistible pull of his thoughts to Emma Rose and the magic they'd shared. What would she say when she saw him? Would this be an agreeable surprise or an awkward occasion? No matter, he would prevail.

If he was honest, a thing he had used to pride himself on, she was one of the reasons he was here. To see the woman who had tilted his grey world into colour again, though she'd only intended it to be for one night. He knew he'd promised just that night but perhaps for a month they might change the rules.

Emma knew Gianni started today.

How could she not? Ten people had told her, as if she were the most fortunate person in Lyrebird Lake. That wasn't what she was calling herself.

He was supposed to be gone for ever. Though, to be honest, had this possibility been at the back of her mind when she'd begun the first of the pre-screening counselling sessions for her mother's genetic heritage? In case Gianni might come back someday? As protection from risking her heart? That wasn't the reason she'd told the counsellor.

Gianni was supposed to disappear into the sunset and never remind her of the incredible world out there for her if she threw the bleakness of her future to the winds.

To top it off, this morning she'd been seconded to Emergency. As a midwife most of her work-load took place in the birthing centre, but today none of her own women were due to give birth, and she was directed to the little emergency ward where a cluster of mini-catastrophes meant the cubicles were full to overflowing.

The worst day in the world to be in Emergency for Emma—Gianni's first day.

She'd barely slept last night, tossed in her bed with a million memories she'd tried to hide from and cross beyond words that he had returned to ruin her good intentions.

Finally, around daybreak, she'd shed her anger at Gianni for his return, anger at herself for being glad, and decided regrets were useless because she could never regret what they had shared. She had stopped tossing and she'd straightened in the bed. Then she'd sat up and squared her shoulders to face the day.

Hopefully their first meeting would be over swiftly amidst chaos and she wouldn't have the time then to dwell on the embarrassment and disaster of his return.

When Emma arrived on the ward, Christine, the much-loved mainstay of Emergency, greeted her like the long-lost second cousin she was. 'Help. Thank goodness. Lovely to see you.' She hugged her. 'Now, your mission today is to get us off on time because this afternoon I have a hair appointment. My man's been home from Africa three weeks and we still haven't celebrated our anniversary.'

'Yes, ma'am. Off in time for hair appointment. And you always look beautiful.' She surreptitiously peeked around for Gianni. Her heart thudded uncomfortably in her throat but she had to believe Christine couldn't notice any difference in the way she was acting. She forced the words out. 'So where's our new doc?'

'Behind that curtain.' Christine glanced around and all seemed momentarily under control. 'Even as a happily married woman I can see that man is a bit of a hunk,' she whispered. 'You could help him finish off and then I'll have him.'

The first Emma saw of Gianni was his bent head, the thick dark hair she'd run her fingers through falling across his forehead, and his dark, bedroom eyes hidden as he bent to suture the torn earlobe of an older lady.

Doris's tranquil face turned sideways towards

Emma from under the green sheet and her eyes twinkled. 'Hello, Emma, dear. I'm being a nuisance as always.'

She felt his swift look but Emma avoided Gianni's eyes. 'Always a delight, you mean.' She smiled and looked at Doris's husband, who sat with arms folded with steadfast concentration as he ensured Gianni did a good job on his wife.

Emma winked at the older gentleman. 'Not the dangerous garden again, Clive?'

''Ear, 'ear,' Clive muttered facetiously. 'She slipped in the mulch and caught her earring on a branch. I think we need to live in a little unit with pot plants. Be nice and safe.'

Emma decided she'd greet Gianni without blushing if it killed her. 'Morning, Dr Bonmarito.'

Gianni glanced up properly and flashed a knee-wobbling grin at her. 'Ah.' As if he'd been waiting for her to look at him. 'Good morning, Emma. Please call me Gianni. I have given you permission to use it.' His voice. That accent. The memories. She fought the warmth that threatened to douse her and at least the blush stopped at her neck.

Thankfully he looked away to his handiwork, cut the last suture and sat back. 'There you go, Doris. As good as new. But you have the bruise behind your ear that will throb when the local anaesthetic wears off.'

Emma winced at the thought, glad to be diverted. 'I'll pop a couple of ice cubes in a disposable glove. Hold it on the swelling on the way home, Doris.' Emma flicked a glanced at Gianni. 'Tetanus shot?'

'No.' He shook his head. 'I think not. The last tango…' He paused as if remembering something pleasant. 'With the garden was only three months ago. Her booster is up to date.'

Then he sat back and looked at her, with a slow, leisurely scan from head to toe, and Emma quickly turned away to concentrate on the pile of discarded swabs. The last tango they'd danced in his chalet made a vivid picture that had nothing to do with ears. Except hers were burning. Not fair.

'I'll clean up here, then.' She glanced towards the other end of the ward and Christine waved and pointed at Gianni. 'I think Christine wants you for her little asthmatic.'

Gianni stripped off his gloves. 'I will move on, then.' He pumped some antiseptic on his hands as he smiled at Doris and Clive. 'Do not battle with branches, Doris.' He rubbed the evaporating gel away before he shook Clive's hand. 'My pleasure meeting you both.'

'Thanks, Doc.'

Doris glanced from the departing Gianni to Emma, and her mischievous eyes gave her away. Emma braced herself. 'Now, there's a handsome young man, Emma. You should entice him to stay and help at the lake.'

Could she entice Gianni? Again? 'He lives

in Italy. And lost his wife in a tragic accident, Doris.'

'Perfect.'

Emma had to laugh at Doris's simplicity. 'He doesn't need more heartache.' She handed the ice fingers to Clive. 'To hold against her ear, Clive.' She helped the older lady up. 'Give me a break, Doris. I travel once a month for the cause and once a week to see Mum. Grace barely sees me and I work the rest of the time.'

Doris opened her mouth for the clincher but Clive forestalled her gently with his hand. 'Here. Put this against the dressing, there, Doris. We should be leaving poor Emma to her work.'

Emma caught Clive's eye and thanked him without words. Doris hadn't needed to say it anyway. It was what she said every time she saw Emma. *Young Grace needs a father.*

Perhaps Gianni would make a good one, if a little strict on propriety. Except where she herself was concerned. How had she been so shameless?

She sighed. What she needed was a relationship with a man that dissolved before she was forty. Then again, she'd tried a twenty-four-hour one and been broken-hearted from that.

Just the thought of Gianni or any man in the same position as her own dear dad made her want to cry. This was why she didn't want love. She'd given up wallowing in self-pity years ago.

She needed to concentrate on her daughter. Grace was her most important concern. To create a world of wonderful memories for her daughter. She needed to stay focussed and plan for the day she might not be capable of being there. Like her own mother couldn't be for her.

Emma glanced at the mess in front of her and cleared her mind of fruitless yearnings. He'd removed his own sharps—good—and hadn't spread himself around as much as most people did when they were suturing. She swept the neat pile of paper litter into the bag hanging off the trolley and sprayed the area with detergent before she wiped it over and put a clean sheet on the bed ready for the next patient.

She glanced back towards the overflowing waiting room. Calling the next person in sounded like a good idea. For her own peace of mind as well as the patients'. But before she could call a name, the automatic doors opened to admit Emma's brothers, both local ambulance officers, and a stretchered patient.

'This way, boys.' Emma beckoned them through to her. Her brothers would ground her, too. Both of them were positive for the gene. Now, that was reality right in the face.

As the busy afternoon wore on Emma remembered why she preferred midwifery to Emergency. The peace and passions of birth were poles away from the adrenalin rush of the emergency department, although a little of the fight-and-flight stuff had come in handy as she'd tried to ward off the onslaught of memories she'd been bombarded with just by working with Gianni Bonmarito.

With weak fascination she'd watched him connect warmly with patients, children, staff, and even the grumpy one-eyed cat one older lady had tried to smuggle into the ward with her own admission, and each positive encounter had made her more aware of what she was missing. And more reason not to short-change him when he'd already suffered in love. The lump in her throat grew to such mammoth proportions she didn't even fancy her lunch.

By the end of the shift Emma couldn't inflict the exposure of more gorgeous Gianni on herself and slipped out the garden door as soon as handover was completed. Lucky Christine was away and rushing home to the man she loved. Emma envied her.

This afternoon Emma would be happy if she

could get to the safety of her house so she could immerse herself in all the good things she held in her life. She needed to batten down the impossible dreams that were beginning to haunt her with ten times more persistence since that morning.

'Our day has been busy.' Gianni's voice brushed over her shoulder like the branch she'd just ducked under. Her neck stiffened and she slowed her steps. Reluctantly she abandoned evasion as a non-starter.

'Very busy.' So much for grand plans, she grumbled silently, but a tiny shiver of excitement disputed her grumbling. Liar. You're pleased to see him, the voice inside her head quibbled. Her lips compressed as she drew in a long breath through her nose, one, two, three, four, and her mouth pursed as she exhaled in a silent whistle and allowed her shoulders to relax.

She saw the branch skim lovingly across his broad shoulders like her own fingers had done a month ago and then he stepped out onto the path beside her. Emma watched the bush spring back. Lucky branch. She glanced at his tousled hair and her hand tightened on her bag in acknowledgement of that fleeting desire to comb it with her fingers. How could she be irresponsibly infatuated so quickly?

Gee, maybe the promise of more mind-blowing sex? that internal smart Alec suggested. Her cheeks burnt and she ducked her head.

He tilted his head at her with a question she couldn't help but see. 'You don't look pleased I have followed you. Would it be better for you if I left you alone?'

She sighed again. It was even more embarrassing her distress showed. 'Look…' She paused. 'Gianni. I'm sorry.' How to tell him? 'It's not you.' She grimaced. 'Well, it is you but it's not your fault.'

He raised his black brows and spread his hands in exasperation. 'There is no doubt it is my fault.'

They'd stopped when they reached the path outside the hospital that ran along the front of the lake.

Gianni needed to cross to the doctor's residence and she needed to follow the path all the way to her house. Alone.

His eyes were on her face, as if searching for the woman he'd held a month ago. 'Of course. You have been let down before? Grace's father?' Now he'd planted himself directly in front of her. 'Can we not be friends, Emma?'

Grace's dad, Tommy, didn't have a mean bone in his body. They'd been children when they'd been together. No. Gianni couldn't be more wrong about the reason she didn't want to tie herself to a man.

But it was still impossible to be mere friends. She raised her own brows and tilted her head. 'Is that what you want to be, Gianni? "Friends" with me?'

His gaze caught hers and the sultry chocolate

of his eyes darkened as they travelled as if to imprint her features on his mind. The sounds of the birds and the swish of the trees overhead faded into the stillness between them.

The air thickened as they stared at each other and Emma felt suspended like a piece of fruit in a jelly. Far too much awareness.

Finally he said, 'No. It is not only your friendship I want.'

She dragged her eyes away to sever a connection that wobbled her knees. 'I thought not.'

He raised his hand to touch her shoulder and hastily she stepped back because then she would be lost. His hand dropped and he frowned down as she tucked her fingers away behind her back. 'It meant something to you, didn't it, Emma? Between us runs a current. You feel it too?'

She could almost laugh at that. Oh, yes. She gave him a sweeping glance of her own. From the top of that thick hair, past his beautiful jawline, across those strong upright shoulders and that chest she'd love to rest her head on again.

She sighed as her eyes fell away. Stop looking. Yeah, well… She swallowed and wished she hadn't indulged. Maybe honesty would work. 'I feel the vibration of you every time you walk past, Gianni, but I can't be interested. I told you that a month ago.'

He went to speak and she lifted her hand to silence him. 'I don't do one-night stands.' She grimaced. 'Except once. And I don't do long term. So where does that leave you?'

He lifted his head and his gaze narrowed. Another silence lay suspended between them and then finally he raised one eyebrow. Wickedly, and her heart kicked out of rhythm.

'Neither short nor long. A leisurely sojourn for the month I am here? Then we would see?' His measured voice raised the gooseflesh on her arms and she couldn't help the mental leap of her imagination to a slow sip of sensation with Gianni.

Wrapped in his arms she'd be safe from the world and the future. Her cheeks burned in case he read the sudden sleepiness in her eyes.

She rubbed her elbows to banish the bumps. What was wrong with her? She rarely thought about sex. Except for every minute for the last four weeks.

She shook her head. Vehemently. Twice. Once for him and once for her. 'I don't think so, Gianni, but thanks for the offer. I have commitments. A daughter and no time.' She couldn't believe she was having this conversation.

He closed the small distance between them again until his chest almost touched hers. Then his eyes drifted down to her mouth. She could sense the brush of an imaginary finger and she had no control over the return of gooseflesh that gave her away again.

His voice dropped. 'So, don't think commitments. Think no commitments. Mutual nourishment in a world separate to our daily lives. I have no time either.'

Suddenly she felt like crying. Then why were they teasing themselves? She threw her head up and gave him a level stare. 'Leave it, Gianni.'

He said, almost to himself but she heard the words, '*Si*. For today.' He leaned forward and kissed her cheek just like she'd kissed his the first day. 'Goodnight, Emma. Sleep well.'

'As if,' she muttered to herself as she walked briskly along the path towards home. Alone.

CHAPTER FIVE

GIANNI stood beside the kitchen table and helped Louisa crumb pieces of veal for their dinner. 'So, tell me about Emma Rose, Louisa.'

'What do you mean?' Louisa glanced up, and her merry eyes even twinkled a little at him. Louisa liked to spoil a man. It made her smile. But she also enjoyed learning the Italian way to treat the veal. This was good.

Gianni returned to his dilemma of Emma and shrugged. 'She won't talk to me.'

'That doesn't sound like Emma.' Louisa's hand stilled as she considered his statement. 'Or do you mean she won't flirt with you?'

Gianni shot a glance at the older lady and then

looked down at the crumbs on his fingertips. 'Perhaps.'

'Ah.' Louisa nodded. 'Emma has issues and if she hasn't told you…' she shrugged '…then really it's not my place to discuss it.'

Some nuance in Louisa's voice warned him. Something that made Louisa sad again. Maybe there was more to Emma's distance than met the eye.

He couldn't prevent the sliver of ice that crept in under his ribs, and suddenly he needed divine reassurance. Please, God, nothing terrible. 'Medical issues?'

Louisa looked out the window to the lake. She sighed. 'I suppose it's common knowledge. Emma's never hidden it.' She met his eyes and at the sympathy in hers the ice around his ribs thickened. 'Emma doesn't believe she can guarantee her future beyond her fortieth birthday. That's when her mother was diagnosed. She's even published her own story to help others.'

Gianni bit his lip to stop himself from asking the obvious question. Surely Louisa would get to the point.

She went on after a long sigh. 'But it all boils down to her belief of her own end.'

He couldn't stand it. 'But what cause? What illness?'

'Huntington's disease.'

Gianni felt the shudder internally if not externally, and suddenly he was staring at the wall opposite and not seeing the picture of a hen scratching the ground. Huntington's? His mind flew back to a patient he'd known very early in his medical career. A young man, early forties, his convulsive arms and legs uncontrolled as he tried to walk.

The mental deterioration that wasn't kind enough to completely remove the realisation that you were helpless and reliant on others until your disease progressed so much you died.

There were lesser degrees, and some of those

with the gene passed away without signs of the dormant time bomb, but the worst-case scenario—the definition reeled off his brain and he murmured it out loud.'Hereditary disorder with mental and physical deterioration, leading to death.'

The bottom dropped out of his stomach. 'Emma inherited the gene?'

Louisa spread his hands. 'I never did understand the genetics, though my late husband tried to explain it. I was always under the impression she did. But that's something you'd have to ask Emma.'

Of course. But perhaps not something you could mention as you ducked under a branch. *Dio.* Poor sweet, adorable Emma. Another sinister thought followed and Gianni winced and looked down at his own steady hand. 'And her daughter? Grace?'

'Aye. The wee one is Emma's main concern.'

Of course. He needed to research. *Adesso.* He washed his hands. 'I will return shortly.'

'Off you go, then. Dinner will be half an hour and I can stretch it for another fifteen if you hit a snag.' Louisa nodded. She understood.

Gianni switched on his computer a few minutes later.

He read up on the disease process for Huntington's to refresh his memory, the statistics of having the gene and the worst-case scenario and, finally, he made a search with Emma's name. Louisa had said she'd told her story.

There she was.

Her photo stared out at him, smiling into his with an apparent serenity that made him ache, the face of Huntington's in Queensland, and her family story.

He read how her mother's diagnosis had been unexpected, a run of early accidental deaths of close relatives had masked the genetic footprints that led to expected diagnosis, and only the progression of the disease, awkward and jerky movements, changes in mood and ability to cope with daily tasks, and the slow deterioration of both physical and mental self-sufficiency had pointed to the answer. One in ten thousand sufferers. Around three hundred and fifty sufferers in Queensland. Was Emma one of those?

His eyes skimmed as he searched for the place where she discussed her own testing and results and couldn't see it. He searched again, and still didn't know whether she'd been tested. But she must have. How could anyone not want to find out?

What he did see were her brothers and that both were positive. Gianni sighed. Cruel fall of the dice for a fifty per cent chance. He eased his neck and stood up. He would eat and return to this site.

The next morning, still bereft of birthing women, Emma returned to Emergency. Today, Emma felt Gianni's eyes on her wherever she walked. There was something different in his appraisal this morning.

Grey smudges darkened his eyes and frown lines came and went on his forehead. He smothered another yawn with his hand. What had he done last night? Had he also had trouble resting or had he been too merrily oblivious to the turmoil he'd left for Emma? She gave up the struggle not to ask. She'd had very little sleep and most of the reason could be laid at the door of Gianni Bonmarito. 'Big night, Gianni?'

His gaze flicked to the empty doorway and back. No patients to distract him. 'I was studying a case on the internet.'

And she'd thought it was because of her and their conversation by the path. Silly girl. 'Was that wise with a work day ahead?'

The gravity in his face as he considered her question made her frown. 'We all make choices,' he said.

Huh? She'd been teasing but apparently his sense of humour was way different to hers. 'You're too deep for me today.' The emergency doors opened and she looked up. 'You need to see these people. This little boy, Lucas, has haemophilia. He's probably had a fall.'

Gianni looked across and nodded. *'Grazie.'*

He strode across in that unhurried walk of his that covered ground with deceptive speed and Emma watched him greet the newcomers. Even with the little exposure she'd had to him she could tell there was something on his mind. Maybe there was someone at his home who'd become sick. She needed to remember he had a family and a life away from here. Another reason it would never work.

She'd decided last night there'd be no happy ending to an affair with Gianni Bonmarito. Even a brief one. It was just that the inner Emma had argued there was no happy ending anywhere, so maybe she should grab what she could of the good life.

But that's what she was doing already. Enjoying her daughter, she'd made fabulous friends in the Huntington's network, had been privileged to talk to those affected from all over Australia, and the community of Lyrebird Lake cared for her like an extra family.

A broken heart was the last thing she needed when she had enough to concentrate on. And she had no doubt her heart would break when Gianni Bonmarito left for Italy because already it ached just looking at him from across the room.

But it was lonely while she waited.

The emergency doors opened and Emma's brothers, Russell and Craig, brought in another stretchered patient. Every time she saw her brothers she winced. Russell, the second of her brothers to test positive for the gene, had now gone on to make a life for himself. Happily married to a wonderful woman, and with genetic help at conception, they planned to have babies in the future. She considered her brothers the bravest people she knew. She just wasn't that brave.

Emma smiled at them but they didn't return it, which made her gaze sharpen. She recognised the patient. Seamus.

Christine's Irish husband. The truck whisperer, they all called him. His rapport with anything mechanical was legendary. He had recently returned from Africa where he'd been paid handsomely to resurrect a rare vintage fire engine for a minor dictator, but it seemed Christine's big anniversary night had been short-lived. Seamus lay with his pale skin blotched with fever and his red hair a damp sweaty mop, tossing on an ambulance stretcher.

His eyes squinted as he groaned in distress and guarded his knees when Emma helped to slide him across to the bed. Joint pain? She stood back and rubbed her fingers where the heat from his body had been absorbed into hers. He was burning up. Ominous, Emma fretted, and glanced at her brothers. 'What happened?'

'We had our weekly fishing trip yesterday and he was fine. Today he's as sick as a dog and he seems even worse now than when we picked him up,' Russell said. 'He didn't have a hope of driving in.'

Emma waved to catch Christine's attention as she began to hook up the cardiac and oxygen saturation monitors.

'Gianni.' Emma's voice carried to where Gianni was chatting with Lucas's mother and he looked up. He too made his way down to the bed.

They both arrived at the same time and Christine took her husband's hand in shock and with her other smoothed his brow. 'What happened? What's wrong?'

'Seamus is Christine's husband, Gianni.' Emma glanced at the other woman. 'Will I take over up there, Christine?'

Christine dragged her eyes away from her man's face. 'Oh.' She blinked worried eyes. 'Thanks. Yes, please, Emma. I'll call you if I need help here.'

Emma left them to it but her concentration was divided between the two ends of the room as she helped ice the swelling above little Lucas's knee from his fall.

'The bleeding under the skin seems to have stopped,' Lucas's mother said.

'Did the doctor say you could go?' Emma picked up the notes and scanned them to see Gianni's orders.

Lucas's mum nodded. 'It stopped sooner than we'd thought it would.' She looked at her husband. 'We probably didn't need to bring him in and waste your time but I always worry when he falls.'

'You absolutely did the right thing.' Emma nodded her head to reinforce the message. 'Never hesitate. Listen to your instinct.' Emma believed that passionately and that went for midwifery, as well. 'A worried mother never wastes our time, and it gave Dr Bonmarito a chance to meet your Lucas without a big emergency.'

The little boy's parents looked relieved. 'As long as you're sure?' They all looked at Gianni down the end of the room. 'He was very good with Lucas. We need more good doctors now Dr Ned has gone. Is he here long?'

'A month, while Dr Angus is away, and then he has to leave.' There was no uncertainty. Emma needed to remember that herself.

The little boy spoke up. 'Can we go home now?' Emma recognised the darting looks Lucas directed at the door and she bit back a smile. He'd had enough. Lucas wanted out of hospital before someone did something to him, like stick a needle in him or put up a drip, which usually happened.

Emma shook her head. 'Soon, buddy. I just need to take some blood first. Is that okay?'

Lucas sighed resignedly. 'I knew it.'

They all smiled and his father ruffled his son's hair. 'Have I told you how proud I am of you today, Lucas?'

Lucas brightened. 'Do I get a treat?'

'You don't have to make your bed this morning,' his mother teased, but everyone knew a treat was in the offing.

After they'd gone, Emma finished up the last of the patients to be allowed to go home and tidied her end of the ward before she drifted back down towards the critically ill Seamus. They'd taken blood, run through two litres of fluid and given paracetamol for the fever and his aches and pains, but there was talk of transferring him to Brisbane if he worsened.

By lunchtime the pathology results were back and as Gianni had suspected Seamus had brought home an infection from Africa. Dengue antibodies were isolated and at least they knew what had caused his fever. The implications for his family were something nobody discounted. Seamus must have incubated the bug since he'd been home and now three weeks later he was sick.

'The real threat is cross-infection to others if he's been bitten by the local mosquitoes,' Gianni told Christine. 'I've seen epidemics like this in disaster areas. In the normal cycle of dengue, the female mosquito feeds on an infected and viraemic human, and in ten days the salivary glands of that mosquito become infected for life. That way the disease is spread to other humans before you know it you have an outbreak.'

He glanced at the wall clock. 'We'll notify the local infectious-diseases department but I doubt they'll do anything with only one case.'

Christine held her husband's hand. 'So how soon will he feel better?'

'It will take a week at least,' Gianni said, 'though sometimes patients can relapse for a few days.'

Emma remembered that adults were more likely to be infected than children, because the town had had a small outbreak a few years ago, but children could become quite ill with the worst forms of the disease. She'd have to watch Grace.

Gianni went on. 'His headaches and muscle pain will probably get worse and he may get gastric symptoms. This part of the disease process has to pass before he'll improve sufficiently to feel normal.'

Christine stroked her husband's forehead. 'Does he have to stay in hospital? Can we do anything for him by keeping him in that I can't do at home?'

'Perhaps not now he's rehydrated, and as you're a nurse. As long as he drinks. He'll be sick and uncomfortable, if you think you can manage.'

Christine looked at Seamus who muttered, 'Let's try home, love.'

Emma touched Christine's arm. 'I'll set up a

roster so someone comes to see you morning and afternoon to give you a hand.' That was how it worked in Lyrebird Lake. If someone needed help, the load was shared through the network of friends, especially with those who worked at the hospital. 'I'll come around in the morning and help with his sponge and changing the bed,' Emma promised.

Gianni continued, 'If he gets worse, ring for an ambulance again and bring him back. We'll set up a room that's isolated. Otherwise paracetamol for the pain and fever. No aspirin or anti-inflammatory drugs because of the risk of bleeding.'

Gianni laid his hand on her arm. 'Keep the insect repellent on all of you. We don't want any mosquitoes that have bitten Seamus biting you. Or your son.'

'Patrick,' Emma said quietly.

Gianni nodded. 'And have Patrick empty any plant pots with water and clear away piles of leaves. No water lying around for mosquitoes to breed in.'

Gianni would have seen this many times in disaster-affected areas. If they haven't already bred, Emma thought, and promised herself she'd check around her own house.

Gianni hadn't finished. He added, 'A mosquito net over Seamus through the day, as well. Remember it is those mosquitoes that feed morning and afternoon that pass on dengue, not the night-time ones.'

Christine nodded. 'I'll get Patrick to see to it.' They strapped Seamus, head drooping, in the passenger seat of Christine's car, and Gianni closed the door for them.

They stood together as Christine and her husband drove off. Emma sighed. 'That's how it spread last time, a teacher back from Indonesia and then through the local insects.' She watched the car drive away with a worried frown. 'Do you think she'll manage? He's a big man.'

Gianni shrugged. 'It is the right of a wife to care for her husband. And vice versa. If he's too much for her to handle then we can care for him here. Or if he becomes more unwell, he'll be transferred out to Brisbane.' They turned to go back inside. 'I think your Christine needs to try, and you seem to have a good support system here.'

'We do.' She stripped the bed and wiped it over. To her surprise, Gianni returned the monitors to their place against the wall and cleared the paper litter. She hadn't imagined he was used to helping nurses. To cover her confusion, Emma rattled on. 'I've spoken to Montana. We'll finish the shift one down but she'll cover Christine's shifts for the next few days with my friend Tammy.'

Gianni helped her tuck the sheet in and then watched her as she slid the new cover over a pillow. 'It is a very efficient service here. I've never worked in a hospital that feels as close knit and supportive as your Lyrebird Lake.'

'Thank you.' She looked at him and could tell he was sincere. No doubt it would be totally different to his work conditions. 'I imagine it's pretty fraught when you arrive at disasters with very little back-up. Here we have Andy for the doctors and the hospital admin, and Montana for the nurses, and they're both great troubleshooters. They've been here since before Grace was born.'

'And one day, your daughter, Grace, she will work here too?' He smiled and she nodded.

She just hoped she was well enough to see that. Emma glanced around the tidy room and realised there was just the two of them now the influx of patients had cleared. 'Cup of tea? Might be a good idea to have lunch—this place is feast or a famine with patients.'

Gianni also looked around and she could see his surprise that the ward was empty. 'You finished everyone. They have gone home? Well done when we weren't looking.'

She felt a little glow from his praise. A glow was safe enough. As long as he didn't touch her. 'You'd written in their notes, so no problem. We're a good team.'

There was a pause as they both thought about what she'd said, and suddenly the banter died. 'Everyone who works here is a good team,' Emma said, and turned away. 'Have you any lunch or do you want to go to the kiosk and buy something? I've brought mine.' Not that she felt like eating. 'I'll watch the door.'

'Louisa has packed my lunch. Like a *bambino*. She gives me fruit, as well.' He shrugged and grinned, and she saw for a moment the small boy he'd been many years ago.

'Lucky you.' Bummer, Emma thought. So much for him leaving for a brief respite. She chewed her lip. Of course Louisa would enjoy looking after a man again. For herself, she wished Louisa hadn't. Five minutes to get her head together would have been very welcome.

They moved to the tea room through an open door adjacent to the emergency entry and both sighed as they sank with relief onto the chairs in the little room.

He was so close. Emma slid across to the far edge of her chair. The space was much too small to sit comfortably with Gianni, Emma grumbled to herself. Strange when she'd had many a pleasant break in here with Christine.

He opened his lunch and bit into a roll with relish. Emma looked at her salad and put the lid back on it. How did you behave normally with a man you barely knew yet knew intimately? Where did she look? What could she say and how could she make her body ignore the fact that he'd touched every inch of her with magic and she him?

She picked up a magazine and fanned herself before she realised what she was doing. Horrified she'd given herself away, she replaced it carefully on the table.

Her eyes slid across to his and he was watching her. With the barest hint of a smile on his face, but it was enough for her to know. Her face flamed.

'Well, it is embarrassing.'

'Si.' His dark eyes softened on hers. 'Perhaps a little.' And he smiled again. 'But delightful.'

She rolled her eyes. 'Great. You find it delightful that I want to sink into a hole in the ground.'

He frowned. 'I have no shame, only if I have caused you distress, and neither should you.' He turned to face her fully, and before she realised it he'd lifted the hand from her lap and clasped it in his. In that movement he could make her feel small and protected. Something she hadn't felt since Gianni had left.

'No,' he said earnestly. 'Shame is not what you should be feeling. You should feel pride at bestowing a precious, healing gift on a man who had no expectation of feeling life again.' He glanced around as if for support. 'You asked me not to contact you. That it was a moment in time for you, so instead I thought of you. Every moment. But in the end I am glad of my chance to see you again.'

Emma looked down at her hand held in his and considered the implications of his statement, and the panic galloped up her throat. 'Let's not talk about this. Here. At all.'

He raised his eyebrows and she could see that wasn't going to happen. She sighed. 'Or at least give me time.' She rolled her eyes. 'I'll need weeks,' she said under her breath, 'to get used to the idea that you came back.'

He let go and sat back. 'Of course. I apologise. You are right. I did not intend to…' He hesitated as if to search for the right word. 'Accost you at work.'

Emma drew in a long breath and changed the

subject. 'So what did your brother think of you coming out here?'

He shrugged and then he sighed. 'I have not lingered at home since my marriage so he is used to me being away. And sometimes the guilt rises because I should see my wife's parents.' There was no doubt he felt his responsibilities. Which seemed strange when he'd spent so much time away from them. 'My nephew will inherit my part of the family lands and businesses if I do not marry.'

His brother might reasonably expect that, Emma thought, after ten years. 'Can I ask what happened between you and your brother?'

He spread his strong fingers and she yanked her eyes away from them. 'His wife did not like me or my rapport with my brother. She succeeded in driving a wedge between us. Now that she has gone, my brother admits that.' There was little visible emotion in his voice, and Emma wondered if he could really be that calm about such a strong subject.

'That's sad. I can only imagine how hard that would be for you both.'

His face was a mask. He needed to learn that sympathy wasn't a dirty word, and she couldn't prevent her hand reaching for his shoulder to squeeze. He lifted his hand and patted hers. 'I do not deserve your kindness. If I had kept my own wife safe, I would have a whole family of my own by now.'

He'd loved her. And now he suffered for years at his own guilt. Life could be so cruel.

Like her father suffered because he loved her mother. Like Emma didn't want any man to love her when her time came. Her eyes narrowed at the tragedy she wouldn't allow. 'Allowing love is a dangerous business.'

Gianni saw the moment when it became personal for her. When the fear to risk love stepped in and she looked to the future. And shook her head.

Now he understood.

It shone from the darker blue streaks in her blue eyes, the denial of any man being tied to the shell of her. Louisa was right. Emma was scared to allow someone to love her. It was her nightmare.

'Like everyone deserves, Emma,' he said softly.

'I think I hear a car coming.' She stood up and walked out the door without looking at him, and his heart ached for her. He'd been so close to telling her he knew her secret. But then what?

And what if she was positive? Could he lose another woman he might grow to love?

No. But how did one stay cold-blooded? How could anybody look into her face, see her courage and honesty, and not want to be there for her? Except she held everyone away.

Emma pushed in an elderly gentleman in a

wheelchair. She'd been right. There was a car and the next two hours were taken up by a steady stream of outpatients with strained ankles, lacerations and croupy coughs.

When the afternoon staff came on she slipped out without saying goodbye and walked briskly away and didn't look back. She didn't need Gianni to see the inexplicable weak tears that made her blink and frown at herself for being pathetic. It was so unlike her not to pull back her shoulders and get on with it.

Today, the short walk along the path under the lakeside trees to her house seemed to last for ever.

Her feet lifted and fell leadenly, her shoulders drooped and the queasiness from lunch returned to disconcert her.

Maybe she was coming down with something, though hopefully not dengue fever. But there'd been several cases of stomach upsets the last two days and that could be what was making her fragile.

Her period was due. She frowned. Was a week overdue, in fact, and her feet paused in mid-stride as she digested the palpitating horror of that thought.

No. She shook her head and patted her chest to quieten her heart. They'd taken precautions. Good ones. Gianni had been assiduous even in the ardour of many heated moments. She had been sure she'd been safe the next day when the first shards of good sense had pierced the euphoria of the morning.

But even the best-laid plans…a tiny voice squeaked in her mind, and her lagging footsteps picked up and she scurried home to check her calendar.

Ten minutes later her car roared out of the driveway on the way to the chemist.

Twenty minutes later Emma perched shakily on the edge of the bath and stared with horror at the second pink line on the test strip. She couldn't be.

By Gianni. A man who lived on the other side of the world in a whole different culture but at this moment in time was here—to see her fall.

She was pregnant.

It was impossible. How could she have two nights of sex in her life and both times she'd fallen pregnant? With a genetic disease hanging over her child. This was her worst nightmare, something she'd vowed she'd never do again, and she needed to think.

Except she couldn't. Her whole world teetered on the craziness of those pink lines in front of her. She stared back again and then dropped the offending strip into the bathroom bin.

One of that two per cent who still fell pregnant despite precautions? No. She screwed her eyes shut and dropped her head in her hands. No, no!

The door banged and a satchel dropped on

the kitchen floor. Routine noises in a day that had turned out anything but routine. 'Mum! I'm home.'

Grace. For a crazy moment Emma scoured the bathroom for somewhere to hide and then she stopped at the ridiculousness of that thought. 'Get a grip, woman,' she muttered to herself. 'In the bathroom, honey,' she called. 'Be out in a minute.'

'Okay.'

Emma heard the fridge door open. Everything seemed louder, clearer as the normal world prepared to disappear for ever.

She needed to tell Gianni. That thought was followed closely by another.

She couldn't tell Gianni.

She couldn't see Gianni because she would never be able to hide her distress.

The tears stung and rolled down her cheek. Another baby and another fear that would consume her. Had she been so wrong to share those few hours with Gianni that she deserved such punishment.

'Mum?'

'Coming, darling.' She scrubbed under her eyes with the tips of her fingers. Then there were the moments of such profound joy with her daughter it was all worth it. Maybe this would prove that way, too. Nothing she could do except love this baby. Too late not to have the test but the result could stay buried. And be put off indefinitely because now three lives would be affected, and she couldn't deal with that, too.

She opened the bathroom door and plastered a smile on her face.

'Hello, darling.' She hugged her daughter, a little harder than usual, drawing what comfort she could for the future. Almost as if she sensed her mother's need, Grace hugged her fiercely back. That love reminded Emma how fortunate she was. The thought was well timed, and she drew a deep breath and let the tension drain from her shoulders. Like she'd learnt to do the hard way—she would worry later.

'How was school, Grace? Did you practise the songs for the play today?'

Grace was big with news. 'My teacher was off sick. She's in the hospital. I lent six people…' her eyes grew big '…even two boys…'

She glanced at her mother for the reaction of that news so Emma made a 'wow' sound before Grace went on.

'My mosquito repellent because the principal said we had to use it at lunch.'

'That was very sensible of you. We don't want anyone else becoming ill, and there could be some nasty mozzies around at the moment.'

'Okay.' Grace wriggled out of her mother's arms. 'I'm going to make a hospital in my doll house in case Barbie or any of her friends get sick.'

'That's a good idea, sweetheart.' Emma

watched her daughter run off happily to her room and wished she too could be so blithely settled in life.

CHAPTER SIX

GIANNI couldn't track Emma for the next week. Missed her by minutes every time he searched, and he knew that she'd arranged it that way.

He was sure Emma hid in birthing as her clients went into labour and he couldn't get away from his own work, snowed under as they were with minor accidents and a slow increase of dengue fever sufferers, to search her out. He was helping to cover the ward work as well as Emergency, with the other two doctors, Andy and Ben, also working long hours. Angus had picked a good time to go away.

When Gianni called on Christine and Seamus out of hours, he found Seamus slowly improved at home again after a brief relapse, but it seemed Emma had only just left. Every time.

On the Friday of that hectic week he glanced at the clock as it edged towards four and decided he'd waited for an accidental meeting long enough. He would search every house in town if he had to.

Then the emergency doors opened and it was Emma. Fortune was finally smiling, he thought with satisfaction, until he noticed the two men, both decidedly unwell, who droopily flanked her.

He frowned. There was something familiar about them and then he recognised Emma's brothers, the ambulance officers he'd seen nearly every day, bringing people into Emergency, in civilian clothes.

'What's happened?' He indicated two beds side by side in the little ward and both men lay down with relief. Tammy covered them with light sheets before she began to check observations. Emma avoided his eyes.

He watched her twist her hands as she glanced from one blond-haired man to the other and not once did she look at him. 'I think it's dengue.' She spoke to the curtain behind his head and he resisted the urge to move into her line of sight. He needed to concentrate on what she was saying, not how she was saying it.

'You know Russell and Craig, my brothers. Seamus and the boys fish together once a week. It seems some mosquitoes have been sharing the dengue from before Seamus came down with it. When I came home this afternoon I found them like this, waiting for me. I'm hoping it isn't the fever but they've both got sky-high temperatures.'

Gianni expected it was. He'd seen a few cases that week and he could make a good guess. He looked at Emma, drank in the sight of her, and thankfully she seemed healthy if a little pale. 'And you? Are you well?'

She nodded. 'So far. I've been using repellent every day since Seamus came in.'

'Good.' Gianni nodded, relieved. 'I, too. We will have to remind those not doing so.' He felt Russell's pulse. 'I'm inclined to agree about their symptoms, but we'll do bloods, of course. We will have the results after lunch. Perhaps you would ring Andy as Medical Director, and he can get onto the media to remind the public about using repellent if he decides. It seems we have an epidemic. We will look after your brothers.'

She nodded, relieved to have something to take her mind off her siblings and the other problem she'd buried deep and wasn't facing, and dialled Andy's number. Before she could get back to see how they fared, another woman and her father came in, complaining of the same symptoms.

By the time Andy arrived, Gianni had assessed three more people with similar symptoms. His dark sculpted face turned grave, and Emma watched as he explained to the senior medical officer about the new cases.

Emma stayed to help Tammy, and both women assessed, treated and transferred patients to the new dengue ward in a previously closed section of the hospital. Always in the back of her mind was the awareness of Gianni. Dark head bent over a frail, grey-haired lady, his capable hands cradling a small child's ankle, his flashing smile as he shook hands on a patient's departure. So tall and caring and clever with his diagnoses, and his orders so clear and concise that working as a nurse beside him could have been a pleasure if it wasn't for the spectre of her secret that hung between them.

She'd avoided him for a week and what had that solved? Nothing. When the rush was over this time she didn't try and slip away without seeing Gianni.

She smiled ruefully at his surprise when she

waited for him at the door. 'It's good to finally see you, Emma.' Gianni raised his black brows. 'I thought you had moved to another planet.'

She gave a strangled laugh. So he'd noticed she'd avoided him. 'I seemed to just miss you all the time.'

'That is what I thought,' he said sardonically. So he hadn't been misled. 'Why don't you come in and say hello to Louisa?' he suggested as they walked out the front of the hospital. 'Tell her about our day. Is your daughter home from school yet?'

'Grace visits her other grandmother tonight.' And Emma's brothers in hospital meant no visitors would drop in. With all that had happened, that seemed too much to bear. She was over being alone with her thoughts.

She didn't meet his eyes. 'I'll pop in and see her. Thank you.' And Louisa would be there to chaperone, she reassured herself. She'd come to the conclusion her weakness for Gianni was worse than the dengue, and she was vibrantly aware of how little a dose of Gianni she needed before her symptoms of infatuation could get out of control.

Darned shame she couldn't find a repellent for that, though the worry of the secret that lay between them was a pretty good deterrent to getting up close and personal.

A week had passed since that momentous afternoon, and she'd arrived at a semblance of calm—in the way of an ostrich—and decided to wait before any decisions were made about sharing her news with anyone. Especially Gianni.

And on Wednesday she'd gone for the last counselling visit because it had already been scheduled and she'd forgotten to cancel. The blood had been taken but the results would be held until the time she might screw up her courage for the truth. Though the confirmation of her pregnancy made her less keen for a decision.

None of that was for discussion, and she'd be

careful. This was just a supervised visit to see how Louisa was.

They crossed the lawn, both intent on their own thoughts, and Emma broke the sombre silence. 'So how is Louisa?' The poignant memories of their first walk to the kitchen seeking the widow settled over them like mist and dampened the afternoon sunshine.

'I think she's okay. She smiles, mostly at my appetite, which is apparently much greater than her late husband's. I must admit she is gifted with food and we are sharing recipes.' He shrugged. 'I think my coming here even for a short while has been an excellent thing for both of us. I feel more settled than I have for a long time.'

Emma turned her face and poked her tongue out at the idea that at least *he* was feeling settled, then looked back at him with assumed calm.

He patted his barely discernible stomach. 'And well fed.' He shrugged his impressive shoulders, and she tried not to remember the feel of them under her hand. 'My life revolved around my work,' he said, then gestured to the lake. 'And this is a whole new setting. Although without the fever patients, it would be more relaxing.'

She had to smile at that and glanced at the vista over the lake. The view shifted her thoughts, thankfully. She had a sudden memory of the lyrebird's song to them that morning with Gianni, and the peace from that moment stole over her.

'I like the people here,' he went on, and she returned to the present. 'Even the sick and their families are warm and friendly.'

His words reminded her of his wonderful manner with patients, and how good she believed he'd be with birthing mums. 'You haven't even had a chance to be with us for a birth yet, have you?'

He shook his head. 'When this craziness with the dengue settles, I hope to have the chance to see you at your work, if I can catch you.' He glanced at her. 'Hopefully I'll get the time before I leave.'

She needed to remember he was going. 'When do Angus and Mia get back?'

His eyes crinkled with his affection for Angus and his wife, and she was surprised at how the ache in her heart pierced deeper. 'They make me smile to see them together.' He shook his head at some memory he didn't elaborate on and then remembered her question.

'Sorry. A little over two weeks. They wish to spend a week in Paris before they come back. They tried to convince Louisa to meet them there. But she will not leave.'

'Paris. Mia will love that.' She guessed Gianni had seen Paris and a lot of other places she hadn't visited. He was in a different league from her. Travel wasn't on Emma's agenda. Especially now.

Maybe in twenty years. When her 'children'

were grown. Oh, God. If she didn't have the gene…

She couldn't imagine such a time but the moment was coming when she needed to face that fear and find out once and for all. But she couldn't do it now.

When they entered the kitchen Louisa looked up with a warm smile at her unexpected visitor. 'Emma. How lovely to see you.' She looked at Gianni and shared her smile with him. 'And how was your day, young man?'

Emma stifled the urge to laugh. 'Young man' made him sound like a schoolboy and he was far from that, though the smile he gave Louisa gave a glimpse of the carefree boy he must have once been.

'We must be fed,' he whispered to Emma, and Gianni moved to the kitchen table and held the chair for Emma, who had no choice but to sit. To Louisa he said, 'My day has been busy, like every day since your stepson left. I think it is a conspiracy to get all of his work out of the way before he returns.'

Obviously Gianni and Louisa had no problem communicating. This was a different side to the man she knew. Where had this playfulness come from?

'Tut. To earn your keep. As you should.' Louisa winked at Emma and turned back to the stove. 'Now, I've just boiled the jug and have scones, fresh from the oven.'

'I will be fat,' Gianni stated as he reached for a scone.

'Pshew.' Louisa looked at Emma. 'He runs every morning along the lake.' She looked at the pile of scones. 'I'll bundle up a few for you to take home, Emma. Keep them in the freezer for guests. Those brothers of yours are always dropping in at your house.'

The conversation turned to Russell and Craig's admission to hospital and the prospect of further cases to come. The health department was sending out an assessor and relief staff were coming in.

Half an hour passed swiftly and Emma realised that, apart from work, she'd needed a dose of the outside world, and conversations other than those repeating in her brain. Slowly, in Louisa's kitchen, she began to feel less desperate and disconnected. She hadn't realised how alone she'd felt in the last week rushing from work to home, obsessed with dodging Gianni.

It was good to sit beside him, buffered by Louisa, having a normal conversation and not living in dread. It was good to see the everyday side to him that Louisa saw.

'It's a crisis for a small hospital like ours,' Emma was saying when the phone rang.

Louisa shoed Gianni away from it as he went to stand. 'Have your tea,' she said.

She answered the phone herself then she looked across at them. 'Yes. Gianni's here and actually

Emma is, too. You want her?' She handed the phone to Emma. 'It's Montana.'

Gianni watched Emma's face, having missed her with an aching need that grated with a rawness he hadn't expected. Now he could see her he felt more settled. Then he saw her frown and glance at him. He hoped Montana's call was not going to take her away from him now that he had finally managed to capture her company.

'I'll come straight away,' she said, and Gianni frowned. There must be something wrong.

'Montana needs a quick hand. A post-partum haemorrhage with a birthing mum.'

'I will come, too,' he said, but he was speaking to Emma's back and he hurried to catch her as she strode swiftly across the grass to the rear of the hospital where the little birthing centre was situated.

When they arrived Montana had removed the new mother from the bath and returned her to bed. It would be hard to tell the extent of a bleed in the bath but from the little he'd seen of her, Montana was no careless attendant and would have moved swiftly at any deviation from normal.

The woman's husband, Trent, sat with his shirt off and his new baby skin to skin against his chest. A blanket lay across his shoulders as he looked on helplessly. Calmly Montana massaged the woman's belly to encourage the uterus to contract.

Post-partum haemorrhage, most often due to the failure of the uterine muscle to clamp down on the richly blood-vesselled bed inside the uterus, could bleed at an alarming rate. The husband certainly looked alarmed, and Gianni could well imagine thoughts that would run through a man's brain as his wife seemed to be in such danger in front of him.

Like watching a woman die from snake-bite miles from any help. Gianni had watched Maria's life slip away, but there was little risk of that here with what was available, so he nodded with empathy to the man as he passed him. 'All will be well.'

The woman, Elise, appeared pale and shocked, and Gianni swiftly inserted the second intravenous cannula that Montana offered him, and took the bloods for the clotting factors and cross-matching she wanted.

Emma loaded and hung the Syntocinon flask, the drug most often used to help the muscles of the uterus contract, and gave ergometerine as a separate injection. Montana continued to rub Elise's uterus though the skin of her belly, and gradually the flow slowed to a trickle and finally stopped completely.

Gianni and Emma's eyes met with relief and Emma slid the blood-pressure cuff over Elise's arm while Montana took the woman's pulse as she looked at Gianni. 'It started slow, so wasn't too bad before we got out of the bath, but it flowed once we made it to the bed.'

'Pulse is ninety-eight.' She stripped off her gloves and brushed the hair out of her eyes. 'Thanks for coming, both of you.'

'No problem. It's always easier with more hands,' Emma agreed, and let the cuff down. 'BP's eighty-five on forty-five, but that should pick up now the other fluids are running in.' Elise smiled feebly and Emma glanced at the woman's husband. 'You okay, Trent?' Emma knew them both from antenatal classes.

He wiped his face shakily with his hand and glanced down at the baby snuggled into him. 'I guess. I just won't look at the blood. And this little bloke seems happy. You guys are amazing. I'm glad we decided to have our baby here and not at home.'

Emma smiled. 'The midwife would have had the same gear in her kit, but it's easier to get help here, certainly.'

Trent nodded. 'I could see Montana had it under control, but more hands do it quicker.'

'And that's enough excitement for today,' Montana said, 'so we'll keep a good eye on Elise to make sure she doesn't do anything else interesting.' She and Emma tidied up around Elise and re-checked her observations before they unglued her new son from his father's chest and shifted him onto his mother.

Gianni stood back and watched the calm and unhurried arrangement of baby and mother and glanced around the now tidy room. This was such a different birth setting from those he had seen in Italy. Very quiet. Very understated with technology, yet prepared, in case help was needed. They'd obviously practised their emergency drills to work so seamlessly and swiftly. He would enjoy learning more about the way the centre, and especially one midwife, worked. He hoped he'd have the chance.

He glanced at Emma as she watched the mother attach her baby to the breast and was surprised to see such a broken look on her face.

His heart clenched at the raw pain he could see, and unconsciously he moved closer to her, but as soon as he shifted the spell was broken. She cast him a glance of pure panic and turned away.

Montana thanked them; it was time for them to go, and they left her and the new parents to enjoy their baby. Gianni regretted that the fragile truce between Emma and himself had somehow been severed. He had the impression she would run from his side if she could.

Once they reached the path outside the hospital grounds he lifted his hand to stay her and she flinched, a reaction that sent the pain from her aversion shooting through him. What was this? What had happened? 'Emma?'

'I have to go,' she said hurriedly, and turned, and as he'd feared she would, she fled. Gianni watched the distance between them grow rapidly, and with increasing suspicion he allowed the wheels in his mind to begin to turn.

Her daughter was away and she would be alone. Perhaps tonight was a good time for Emma and him to talk.

Emma knew Gianni would come. Would find her while she was by herself. She contemplated briefly visiting Montana or Misty so that he wouldn't speak to her while her defences were down. Because that was what had happened today.

She bunched the hair on the back of her head into her fists and closed her eyes. It was all so complicated and tragic, and she was sick and tired of the endless circles that had been spinning in her head for a week.

Of the subterfuge of avoidance, which had been difficult enough while she'd had birthing women but would be impossible when she had to work in Emergency.

It was time to be open. She wasn't a coward and despite the complications he might prove to add, she felt she had no right to keep Gianni in the dark about his own child. She'd just needed time to get it straight in her own head first.

It might have been easier if she didn't like and admire Gianni. If like was all it was. She was so aware of him. So attuned to his thoughts and his moods and his intentions that she suspected there was more than like involved. But she couldn't love him. Had promised herself she wouldn't fall in love. Had been so sure little harm could come of letting down her guard once. Well, she knew better now.

When Emma opened the door, Gianni couldn't help notice the skitter of panic in her blue eyes and wondered how he had caused such negative emotion in this woman, the last person he wished to hurt. It seemed there was a lot for them to discuss.

But he would go if she wished. 'Will you speak with me, Emma?'

'Come in,' she said, though the words didn't echo her actions because she didn't step back immediately to allow entry. Perhaps it was too much to ask. He hesitated but then she did move away from the door and turned and walked from him into the house. Immeasurably relieved, he followed.

He'd been under the impression they'd agreed to think only good things of what had lain between the two of them but something was wrong. Something had changed.

Emma stopped in the family room and turned to face him but didn't sit down as she hovered indecisively in the middle of the room. 'Why are you here, Gianni?'

'Why?' He tried to understand her mood. The mixed signals she sent and the emotions in her blue eyes. He realised that reading unspoken sentiment from women was not something he was skilled at. 'Because something is wrong.

Why are you afraid of seeing me? Talking to me? Afraid of me?'

She sighed and he heard the weight of exhaustion in her voice. She sounded so tired. What was wrong with Emma? Was there some other medical condition he knew nothing of?

She lifted her hand and held her throat. 'I'm not afraid of you, Gianni. At times when I'm with you I feel the safest I've ever felt.'

His breath eased out. He'd been unaware he'd been holding it as he'd waited. It was amazing how good that admission made him feel. Perhaps dangerously so. 'Then what is the matter between us?'

He could read the struggle in her eyes and the indecision that crossed her face but not the cause. Then she said it. Baldly, and it was the last thing he expected. 'I'm pregnant. We're pregnant. Despite the precautions we both took.'

He could feel the shock reverberate through him like a seismic wave inside his chest. Something he'd never expected to be faced with because he'd prided himself on his care. Pregnant. A baby. It couldn't be.

He shook his head at the idea. 'We took good precautions.'

She sighed. 'That's what I thought.'

'There has been no one else?' He regretted the words as soon as they left his mouth but they needed to be said. He'd been duped in the past. Couldn't help the knee jerk of disbelief that Maria's final truth had left him with, but he regretted the spasm of pain that crossed Emma's face. It seemed the answer was no.

Her voice was barely audible but the words were clear. 'I'm not going to have a slanging match with you, Gianni. But don't…' She paused as if to control herself. 'Ever doubt me again.'

'My apologies.' He could hear the stiffness in his own voice but his mind was reeling. He did not dispute that he'd enjoyed their brief affair, and since then what little time he'd spent with

Emma, but for life? To share a child? With a woman he barely knew if perhaps not barely in the biblical sense. Speaking of which, he didn't even know her religion—and now his child was involved. If they moved to Italy, perhaps she would convert.

Now was not the time for choices or decisions or paths to choose. The path was there and he would take it. And so would she. It was the correct thing to do.

'We must be married.' His voice was resolute.

'Spare me,' she muttered, and in shock he realised that the answer was no foregone conclusion. The unthinkable slapped him in the face. She was going to refuse. And did.

'A proposal? No, thanks.'

He straightened. 'It is the only thing to do.'

'It's not that simple.' Now she did sink down onto the couch, as if her legs no longer supported her, and he sank down next to her.

'I have a daughter who doesn't know you.' She gestured to the simple room. 'A family, a place I love.' She looked at him with narrow eyes. 'And work I love and spent my teenage years making possible. I can manage here with another child. I've already proved that.'

She threw her hand out toward him. 'You? You are passing through, have come from another continent.' She drew a deep breath as if to steel herself. 'And I have a disease that made me promise myself I would never marry. You need a woman who can provide your family with a bloodline.' She shook her head. 'That woman isn't me.'

So she had tested positive. The blow landed and he barely absorbed it. He waved his hand. All that could not matter. He was the father of this child. And then the ramifications of her statement sank in. 'Do you know that for sure? Have you really tested positive for the gene?'

He saw the moment when she realised he knew

her secret. The shock, the idea of his acceptance, the disbelief that he understood. All reasons she'd put the barrier between them.

Now he understood. Poor Emma. Dear, sweet, Emma. 'Still, I would be there for you and our child.' He paused as he remembered that not only Emma was involved. 'Children.'

It was worse than she'd imagined. He'd be there. He'd sacrifice his life because he had a stake in the child she was carrying. He wasn't in love with her and, please, God, she wasn't in love with him. They were pregnant but it didn't mean he had to be doomed. It didn't have to be.

'Don't you see? Either I have the gene, and Grace and this child are at risk as well, or I haven't got the gene and my life is still to be here for the people I love who have not escaped. My life is here and yours is elsewhere.'

So it was not set in stone. 'Then take the test.' He shook his head, bewildered. 'Of course, take the test. I do not understand how you have not already. But now there is more reason.'

She shook her head vehemently. 'There is more reason not to.' She put her head in her hands. 'You have no conception.' She looked up. 'Ironic word choice.' Then she shook her head. 'The fear that if I test positive, Grace also has that chance. It would destroy me. I couldn't live with that. And now a new child. Perhaps Grace is free but then this, our child, could prove positive. How would I cope with that?'

'I would deal with that as it comes. As your husband. I would be there for you. All of you.'

'No, you won't.' The cry came from her heart. Just like her father. Anguished. Devastated. 'You can't.'

He shrugged in the old way. 'Too late.'

She shook her head, almost wildly. 'I will not do to you what my mother unwittingly has done to my father.'

He said slowly, 'You are so sure you have the

Huntington's gene—and this is why you haven't confirmed it?'

She looked away. 'Yes. Every day. Every time I forget something. Every shake of my hand. And I wonder if this is the start. I don't want to share my life with someone who has to watch that. I've chosen to do this alone, and I don't want to change that.'

Was that the first lie she'd told him? He didn't know why he doubted her. Perhaps it was his own wishful thinking but something told him she wasn't sure. But she was in no state to argue with.

'It does not change things.' He shook his head. 'How do you know your father would not refuse to exchange the bad years because of the good years he enjoyed with your mother? The ones that came before?'

'Nobody could.'

He tried to hold her hands but she wouldn't let him. Twisted away from him. He lowered his voice but his intensity did not lessen. 'Perhaps you should ask him.'

She looked at him, bitterly. 'I don't have to. I know I wouldn't.'

'I don't believe you.' He caught her fingers finally. And held them. 'Marry me, Emma. Let me be a part of our child's life. A part of your life and Grace's.'

'No.' She shook her head. 'But I owed you the truth about my pregnancy.'

It was his pregnancy, too. He tried to make her look at him but she kept turning away. 'You are having my child.'

She spoke to the floor. 'Don't make me wish I'd never told you.'

Why was she like this? 'It is too late for that. And I would have discovered.' He caught her eyes and raised stern brows. 'You would not have liked the consequences of that.'

She tossed her hair. 'You are not the lord

of your little village here, Gianni. You don't frighten me.'

He raised his brows. 'Then why have you waited to tell me this? You must have known for days. A week?'

She put her head in her hands. 'Why do you think? What if we have created another sufferer to live the life and lies that I have lived? Like my poor baby, Grace, could be.'

He understood. Gianni felt the weight fly from his shoulders. The lifting of a stone the size of a statue, and suddenly breathing was much easier. He would see that she took the test. It would change everything. Not that it would change his proposal. He would make her understand.

To a plan, then. 'It is time I became acquainted with your daughter.'

He saw her arrested attention and the way her eyes narrowed. 'I don't think so.'

'I beg to differ.' He stood up. 'But I will give you time to get used to the idea.'

CHAPTER SEVEN

EMMA didn't see Gianni over the weekend as she spent most of her time between her brothers at the hospital and two picnics with Grace in difficult-to-access places. All designed to give her space to think of Gianni's unexpected suggestion.

When she was out of his influence she could think more logically, and the more she thought of Gianni's proposal the less sensible the idea seemed.

Monday, Tuesday and Wednesday conspired without Emma's help to keep them both busy in separate wards, and suddenly it was Thursday and almost the end of her first shift in Emergency since she'd brought her brothers in.

Emma mused out loud as she glanced at the clock. 'Only an hour to go?' Gianni didn't answer and Emma smiled to herself wryly. He was giving her the silent treatment because she wouldn't invite him to tea with her and Grace.

She guessed that was the reason but she wasn't asking. Apart from his request early in the shift and her refusal, it had been quite peaceful that morning. The opposite from what she'd thought it would be like when Montana had asked her to do the shift with Gianni.

He was too quiet. She wasn't sure what he was up to but he'd been nowhere near her, not easy in a small ward, and Emma had found her own glances drifting towards him at the other end of the room.

Maybe he was having second thoughts about pursuing her and had realised it wasn't going to do him any good. That would make her life easier. Or maybe he'd just changed tactics.

Emma wasn't sure she liked the uncertainty but she guessed that was the idea—to annoy her.

The tension had risen a little as their shift was drawing to a close, and she hoped the afternoon staff arrived on time and she could slip away.

Today it was noticeable that the flow of dengue fever sufferers had finally lessened because the shift had progressed at a more leisurely rate, though with each new patient suspicious symptoms were still checked.

When a plump woman, Juliette, arrived with abdominal cramps and a swollen belly, she was examined with the fever in mind. But she didn't have a temperature or a headache.

'The pain's in my belly, bad pain, and it gets excruciating in my back.'

'Is it constant?' Gianni palpated the lumpy abdomen.

'It comes and goes,' Juliette whispered as another pain began to grab her.

Emma frowned at the familiar words. She

looked at Gianni as he spoke to Juliette, and moved closer, but before she could say anything Juliette turned suddenly wild eyes to Gianni and grabbed his shirt collar. 'I have to go to the bathroom, quick.'

She'd heard that before. That was when suspicion crystallised for Emma and Gianni wasn't far behind her.

He looked down at Juliette's belly and his hand followed. 'Her abdomen's as tight as a drum now,' he said, and glanced at Emma with raised eyebrows before he edged the stethoscope down from Juliette's umbilicus to her pelvic bone. Suddenly he stopped.

'There it is! Distinct and unmistakable.' His eyes met Emma's and for the first time that morning he smiled.

He offered her the stethoscope and Emma bent down to listen. The unmistakable sound of a foetal heartbeat could be heard galloping along merrily inside his mother.

'It seems this lady's for you.' He turned to Juliette. 'It appears your baby has decided to arrive.'

Juliette turned hysterical eyes to Emma as she tried to edge her way out of the bed. 'What's he talking about?'

Emma moved in closer so she could speak quietly. 'You're having labour pains. Did you realise you were pregnant? I think you might want to push.'

Juliette shook her head and bit her lip. A spasm of pain not related to her physical symptoms crossed her face. 'How could I be pregnant?' She looked from Emma to Gianni. 'That's cruel. We can't fall. Both of us are sterile.'

'It seems you're not. We both heard the baby's heartbeat,' Emma said gently but with feeling. 'You poor thing. It's a shock you'll have to get used to because I'd say it's all going to happen quickly.' She glanced around. 'Did anyone come in with you?'

Juliette's eyes widened. 'My husband. Ron.'

'I'll get him,' Gianni said, and she and Emma glanced at each other.

'How's that going to go?' Emma asked.

'Disbelief. It's a miracle. But he'll be in shock. Like I am.' The woman screwed up her face and held her breath. 'You sure I can push?'

Emma lifted the sheet and the sudden pop of the bag of waters flooded the bed with clear liquid. 'I'd say yes.' She reached for a pair of gloves and helped the woman out of her underclothes. None too soon.

As Gianni and the new father arrived, Juliette let out a scream that would no doubt raise the hair on the back of her husband's neck and a little dark head appeared between the woman's legs.

Swiftly the baby's shoulders slid out, then the belly and finally feet all tumbled into Emma's hands in a gush of warm amniotic fluid and three coils of cord.

'Good grief.' Emma smiled at the woman. 'For someone who can't have babies, you're darned good at it.'

'Oh, my.' Juliette blinked down at her baby and blushed bright red as she remembered how noisy she'd been. 'I'm sorry I yelled.'

Emma wiped his face with the sheet. The little boy screwed his nose up, coughed, scowled in the general direction of his mother and father then threw back his matted head and roared. Emma exchanged glances with Juliette and smiled. 'A scream like that is a "let's move this baby" noise, and did the job beautifully,' Emma reassured her. 'And now it's his turn. You're both amazing.'

Emma met Gianni's eyes and the amusement there made her own lips compress as she tried not to laugh. Gianni passed Emma a towel to dry the baby's head and chest before she handed him to his mother, and within moments her son was snuggled against her skin with a blanket over both of them.

'Afterbirth now,' Emma murmured as she bent down, completed the job and then straightened.

It was over. A very low-key birth, except for that one scream of fear, incredibly short and wonderful, and if not for Juliette's cry even the people in other cubicles would have been unaware of the drama.

'A baby was born,' Emma said, and smiled. That was when the new father fainted into Gianni's arms.

Gianni was watching Emma, admiring her calm acceptance of the natural order of birth and enjoying her delight. He hadn't noticed the pre-sway of the fainting man. But instinctively his arms closed around Ron and lowered him gently to the floor. Ron stirred and groaned.

Emma slid a pillow off one of the other beds and under Ron's head and handed him a damp washer to wipe his face. 'Stay there for a minute, Ron.'

Fifteen minutes later both parents had been wheeled over to Maternity with their son and Gianni and Emma were writing up notes.

Gianni grinned down at his notes and shook his head. He looked at Emma as she concentrated on her transfer sheet. To witness such a birth was auspicious. 'There must be something in your water around here. Such a fertile place.'

Emma swung her head around but no one was close enough to hear. 'Don't start.'

'But that couple were delightful. We have to celebrate their son's birth. One must celebrate miracles.' Gianni attempted a helpless shrug. 'Louisa is out for dinner tonight at Montana's. That is also a sign you should come out with me.'

She did not look convinced. 'No, it isn't.'

'Oh, yes. Though perhaps it is a divine sign you need to invite me to dinner at your house.'

Emma shook her head but he knew she was trying not to smile. This was better.

The morning had been fraught with silences. Silences he'd made as he'd racked his brain on ways to get her to allow him into her life. Silences when he had begun to despair of penetrating the barriers she'd erected since he'd last seen her. And barriers he feared would become even more insurmountable as time went on.

'That wasn't the sign I read,' she said, and slid the chart across to him.

He signed the medication order she'd written up for after the birth. 'Perhaps you did not see the sign that said I would *bring* dinner?'

She narrowed her eyes at him. She was tempted. He knew it. She pursed her lips. 'I may have seen that one.' Grudgingly.

His heart lightened. 'Do I need to bring enough for your daughter?'

'Absolutely. And she's fussy. I won't have to cook at all.'

Good. But he wasn't crowing in case she changed her mind. 'No problem.'

Gianni arrived at six as instructed. It seem very early to him but he did not eat with an eight-year-old usually so that must be why. He knocked again on the door.

'Hello, Dr Bon-mar-ito,' Grace said. She opened the door and stood back. 'Mummy is in the kitchen.'

'Please call me Gianni. If I may call you Grace?' He handed her the foil-wrapped garlic bread and kept the wine swinging on his arm in a bag.

He'd brought a casserole dish with the main course in it and a bottle of non-alcoholic Lambrusco that he'd found for Emma. The aroma of the pasta had been teasing him since he'd put it in the car. Good choice, his stomach said.

'What's in the dish?'

'My special spaghetti Bolognese recipe that I am famous for.' And he'd never met a child that didn't like Bolognese. He mentally crossed his fingers.

'Yum. Though usually Mummy makes it.'

'This time we will give your mother a rest.'

Grace looked at him gravely. 'Good. She's been tired this week.'

Gianni looked at this serious little girl in front of him and nodded. His fault. 'She is lucky to have a daughter who can see this.'

Grace considered his words and then shrugged. 'This way.'

Gianni followed her and when he found Emma setting the table in the big open kitchen he searched for the tiredness her daughter had noticed. Emma's cheeks were flushed and she didn't quite meet his eyes. Not too tired at this moment.

'Hello,' Emma said to the wall behind his head

before she bent down to help Grace. 'That smells good.'

'Bisgetti Bolonose,' Grace said and handed her mother the bread. Emma smiled as she took the loaf.

'And garlic bread and wine.' Emma didn't correct her as she looked at Gianni. 'Wow. A party.'

Grace looked up at Gianni. 'Did you know it was Mummy's birthday?'

Gianni blinked. He looked at Emma? 'It is?'

'Twenty-five today.'

'Well, you can have the non-alcoholic wine and Grace and I will wash up afterwards.'

She laughed and he was glad to see it. No. She didn't look tired at the moment. And when he had a chance he would order a cake to be delivered. No doubt the Lakeside could handle that.

'I'll get the good glasses from the den,' Emma said, and as soon as she left Gianni bent down to Grace. The child he had no idea how to connect with. Though they had one thing in common. 'Have you any balloons? And some ribbons?'

Grace nodded and dashed off, returning within seconds with three balloons and two red ribbons in her hands. 'Grace is going to show me the yard,' he called out to Emma, and the two of them slipped out the back and around the corner.

'If I blow them up, we can tie them to the ribbons and hang them above the table.'

Grace nodded and her eyes were shining. 'I made a card. At school. I forgot.'

'That is good. A cake will come after our dinner.'

Three quick balloons later, Grace and a slightly red-cheeked Gianni returned to the kitchen with their gaily ribboned balloons and Gianni tied them to the fan on the ceiling so that they hung down over the table.

'What's this?' Emma smiled at the balloons as she came back into the room. Grace produced the card she'd left in her satchel. 'Thank you, darling.' Emma kissed her daughter for her effort.

'I blew up the balloons.' Gianni tilted his cheek and to his relief Emma deigned to give him a peck, too. It was a good start to the evening. He could only go forward.

'Would you like to see my Barbie dolls, Gianni?' Grace had turned serious again. 'I could bring the house.'

Barbie dolls? Gianni looked at Emma, who tried to hide her smile. 'Certainly. I have never seen a house with Barbie dolls.'

'I'll bet you haven't. Barbie dolls,' Emma clarified while her daughter was out of the room. She gestured with her hands. 'Dress-up figurines,' Emma said as Grace ran to find her plastic friends. Emma put the casserole dish and the garlic bread in the oven to reheat and tried not to see the wicked glint in his eyes.

'Ah. Perhaps you have something you wish to show me, too?'

Emma raised her brows and refused to be drawn. 'No. I'm fine, thanks.' Gianni smiled slowly but didn't move any closer and the heat came from somewhere other than the oven.

Grace returned with her box of Barbie dolls, who all seemed to be either mothers or midwives as they were introduced, and Gianni laughed and asked if there were any boy dolls or, heaven forbid, doctors among the housemates.

'Of course. We need doctors, too. If you're sick, silly. Sara-Jane is a doctor.' She held up a scantily clad brunette. 'She's on her days off at the moment, though.' Grace sat down beside the house and drifted into Barbie land as she rearranged and fell into conversation with one of the dolls.

Gianni looked at Emma with amusement. 'I see your daughter understands the concept of a shift-working family.'

'And the concept of finding her own amusement. She's had to learn and I don't think it's a bad skill to have.' Emma turned to Grace. 'We're going to sit on the veranda and have a glass of wine. Would you like to bring your house outside to play?'

'No, thanks.' Grace was immersed.

She returned her attention to Gianni. 'Could you do that as a child? Amuse yourself?' She gathered the glasses and he brought the wine and held the door for her. They smiled at each other at the expected courtesy.

'*Si*. My brother and I had many possessions but not the advantage of extra company,' he said as he followed her out. 'We both had good imaginations.' There were two wooden chairs side by side with a table between them and the view across the road and over the lake was framed in green leaves from the overhanging trees.

'You have a beautiful view.' He could see

across to the trees on the other side of the lake from there.

'Yes.' Emma sighed. 'It was hard for my father to leave here but my mother needed a higher level of care than was available in Lyrebird Lake or even somewhere close enough to travel to.'

He returned his gaze to Emma and he found the view even more attractive. 'How long has your mother been in care?'

Emma still stared unseeingly across the water. 'For six years.' The breeze lifted the fair hair across her nape.

Gianni watched her profile until she turned. 'And your father stays with her?'

Emma nodded. 'He rents a small flat in Brisbane and visits every day. I go up most weekends except when I work.'

Gianni could see Emma hated it that her father, to her mind, was trapped. 'And Grace? Does she understand why her grandmother is away?'

'She knows that Nana's hands shake.' Emma

glanced back towards the kitchen and her daughter. 'And that she drops things and sometimes her hands fly out. She knows that sometimes Nana isn't as happy as other times but she accepts that. We talked about Nana being Nana and her illness will get worse and the doctors are working on a cure so other people won't get sick like Nana.'

The door opened and Grace was standing there. A smaller blonde edition of her mother and very serious. Emma lifted her arm and Grace came in under it and climbed on her lap for a cuddle. 'I heard what you're talking about,' Grace said.

Gianni bit his lip but Emma didn't seem perturbed. It made him admire her all the more. 'That's okay, Grace. Gianni was asking about Nana and why she lives in the hospice.'

Grace nodded and leaned towards Gianni with her little face lifted to his in earnest. 'It's like.' She paused and thought about it. 'If someone stole my Barbie house, it would be gone. But this disease is stealing Nana's brain one Barbie at a time. And you don't get the dolls back so the house is getting emptier.' She lifted her chin. 'But I still love the house and can remember the fun I had with each Barbie, even though it's gone.' She sighed and sank back into her mother's arms, which tightened around her.

Gianni blinked, because for the first time in a very many years he allowed the emotion to rise in his throat and sat in awe of these two amazing beings. 'I see that. Thank you, Grace. That is a very good way of explaining.'

The timer on the oven rang and Grace climbed off her mother's lap with a child's resilience. 'Dinner's ready. I'll put the house away now.' She ran off and the screen door banged as she let it close behind her.

'Does she know that you're at risk? And her?'

Emma lifted her barely touched glass and stood up. 'She's asked. I've said that the chance is the same as having a boy baby or a girl baby. Nobody knows until it happens or they're tested. We haven't gone further than that.'

His eyes narrowed. 'If you had the test you could stop your worry that Grace will be at risk.'

She lifted her chin and dared him to argue. 'If I had the test I could find out just how real that risk is.'

He wanted to know now. About Grace. About Emma. About his own unborn child. Not wait for some nebulous time for Emma to feel it was right, but he curbed his impatience and tried to see it from her position. He sighed. He couldn't.

He could tell she was finished with the topic and for the moment he accepted that. She'd been more open than he'd expected and he had a lot to think about. These were all issues they needed to explore if he wanted a part of his child's life, and he appreciated her honesty.

They stood and he opened the door for her, and the tempting aroma drifting from the oven flowed over them. Regardless of those dilemmas, they all had to eat. The world continued to turn. 'Grace said she likes Bolognese.' His way of agreeing to drop the topic.

'We both do.' She smiled at him and he savoured the beginning of the first sign of acceptance he'd had from her. Except for the physical that neither of them seemed to have much control over. A tiny acceptance but a beginning.

Two hours later it was time for Grace to retire and Gianni was shown the door. 'Thank you, Gianni.' Emma's cheeks were flushed and they'd all laughed a lot. 'It was a lovely birthday.'

He waved his hands. 'I would have liked to have brought a gift.'

'You did. Grace enjoyed your company and so did I.'

He could see that and it warmed his soul more than he would have believed possible. He'd seen the maternal side of Emma tonight and she shone at it. 'That is good. Because I have to go up to Brisbane for the weekend, and I'd like to come with you to meet your parents.'

Her smile died. He watched it fall off her face like a napkin off their party table but he refused to regret the request. 'Why?' she said.

So afraid. 'Because I've heard that you have your mother's eyes and your father's strength. Because you won't let me in for the reason of how their life is.' Because he needed to understand this woman and perhaps her parents were a clue.

He was beginning to read her frown, the thoughtful purse of her lips. And occasionally the nuances of her smile. All things he hadn't noticed in a woman in a long time, and the practice had become addictive.

She tossed her hair. He'd noticed she did that, too, but, it seemed, only around him. Good. He was glad. No hair tossing around other men would keep him happy.

'What if I don't want you to come?' she said.

He could feel the pull at the edge of his mouth as he shrugged. 'Then I must persuade you.'

Her eyebrows went up. 'Do you think you can?'

'Certainly.' Of course.

Emma had to laugh. She'd done a lot of that tonight. It would 'certainly' be a different week-end if Gianni was around. She looked at him, tall and debonair despite the casual clothes he'd chosen, casual but still elegant in an expensively masculine way.

She tried to see his motive for wanting to meet her parents but the feeling of lightness he'd generated with his company blinded her and it was too hard at this moment to look for reasons why she should bar him from his desire. 'Suit yourself. Lucky that you have your own things you have to do because my weekend is pretty busy.'

He turned to Grace. 'Are you coming this weekend, Grace?'

Grace yawned and shook her little blonde head. 'Grandma is taking me to the circus.'

CHAPTER EIGHT

SATURDAY arrived and Emma dropped Grace off at her paternal grandmother's with her rolling Barbie suitcase trailing behind her. It bumped and clattered as Grace skipped up the curving path in her pink sundress to where Tommy's mother waited. Grace waved as her mother drove off.

As she glanced back Emma felt as though a part of her life had receded in the rear-vision mirror. This morning's phone call had seen to that.

Now she regretted Gianni's push to see her parents today. Who knew what she'd been thinking when she'd said yes to dinner out and staying in Brisbane for the night? She didn't know why she'd agreed, perhaps because she felt guilty that she'd refused his proposal, but she made the proviso of her own room at her own expense. In the cold light of day she wished she hadn't agreed to go with him at all.

And now this morning's notification had changed everything. Tomorrow she would find out. The next time she saw her daughter she'd be a different woman, if she could bring herself to attend.

If she did, she would know finally what did or didn't lie in store for them with the Huntington's gene, because the results were irretrievably back. But not irretrievably opened, and they kept telling her she still had that choice.

The ramifications of what lay inside an envelope sent cold shivers down her back and she didn't know if she could sit in front of the woman who'd become her friend over the three counselling sessions she'd needed before this impending consultation.

She drove home and parked her car in the garage. She sat in the semi-darkness for ten minutes before she shook herself and moved to the veranda to wait for Gianni.

How she wished she'd never agreed to drive up to Brisbane with him. It was a mammoth dilemma. But how to get out of his company without explaining why she wanted to be on her own?

The specially organised appointment by Andy's friend, the genetic counsellor, was on Sunday at noon. Her brain had frozen and when Sunday had been offered she'd realised she'd still be there, with Gianni, and had said yes.

There with the last person she felt ready to share the news with because either way she was going to lose.

If it was positive then the waiting began all over again until Grace, let alone this new, unborn child inside her decided to have their own tests.

And for the first time she really thought of what would happen if it was negative. While she herself would be free of the spectre, she wouldn't be free of the guilt that she'd been spared. That freedom meant she would be there to watch others she loved go through what her mother was going through and she would never leave them to manage alone.

Every day she'd avoided the end of not knowing. Of having no choice but to accept her fate. The fate of Grace. And now the fate of Gianni's baby. And by proxy the fate of her love for Gianni. But she didn't want to know.

It hadn't been until that morning had dawned that she'd suddenly realised she hadn't factored in her feelings should the result be negative, and there was no time to think. It was all too much.

She saw his car pull up and his stride up the path. She watched him walk under the rose arch with a strange detachment in her eyes that allowed her see him as a whole.

A tall, imposing man with an aura that spoke of quick decisions and swift action. To think she'd run her hands over those broad shoulders and lean, corded muscles of his body and he'd crushed her too him against his solid chest and made her heart rate speed frantically like the pedals of a pushbike downhill.

Lithe, and light on his feet, he was beside her in an instant. His brows furrowed.

'What is wrong, *cara*?' Gianni paused as he looked down, his thick brows creasing as he studied her face.

She stood, suddenly overwhelmed that this man had decided to spend his life with her not because he loved her but because she was pregnant with his child. That was a reality she couldn't escape.

He'd been more determined, not less, when she'd disclosed her family history, all because of an accidental pregnancy. Not because he couldn't live without her.

But she could never accept, regardless of her Huntington's result on Sunday, because her future was firmly in Australia. She would be either caring for family or being cared for by them. That was why she hadn't told him the result was pending. Horribly imminent.

'Nothing wrong,' she said, and walked towards the car. Gianni carried her bag.

When he opened the car door for her, Gianni's eyes narrowed at the paleness and tension in her face. He'd planned this trip to the last detail and his plans to woo Emma finally now appeared less secure. 'Did you not sleep? Is Grace unwell?'

'Good morning to you, too, Gianni.' She did not look too pleased with his solicitous comment and he searched her face again for clues.

'Grace is fine.' She slid into the car and he shut

her door, his brow creased as he walked around and climbed in himself.

She sighed. 'I'm sorry. I'm a little flat this morning and not very good company. I didn't sleep well.' She buckled her seat belt and stared straight ahead. 'And unless you'd like to take separate cars, I just want to get it over with.'

This was new territory. And not like the woman who embraced life and hurt no one. He tried to fathom the new source of her distress but he was still lacking the skills.

'Get the visit to your parents over with?' He did up his own seat belt. 'Or perhaps the idea of spending time with me as a whole is exhausting?' He reached for the key and then sat back again to face her. 'Perhaps you could tell me what I have done to offend you?'

She did look at him then and bit her lip 'You've done nothing wrong.' The sincerity in her voice allayed some of his misgivings. 'Please. I'm tired and don't want to talk about it.'

He had to offer. 'Would you prefer to take your own car?' He saw the colour flood her face and he hid his disappointment. Yes, she would.

Emotions, many and varied, chased across her face and he wanted to draw her into his arms and comfort her for whatever new thing had caused this upheaval, but the way she held herself demanded he not invade her space. He ran his hands through the back of his hair. He spent so much time trying to fathom this woman he was sure he'd missed many opportunities to do what he wished to do.

'Take my car? I don't know,' she said. 'So let's go.'

At least she hadn't decided yes. He'd felt obliged to make the offer but he wouldn't give her another opportunity to change her mind. He turned the key in the ignition and pulled away from the kerb with little delay.

It had been very close but he still had the woman he wanted in the seat beside him. He reached and turned on the car's sound system and the soft strands of *Tosca* filled the space between them. He saw her sink back in the seat, her shoulders dropped and she closed her eyes. Good.

Emma slept, her face unworried in repose, and he was thankful for another reason she hadn't driven herself. It was his duty to keep her safe and as the black beast swallowed the miles to Brisbane Gianni thought about the last month. He thought of all the high and low points of a very strange courtship with this woman who'd so easily assailed the barriers he'd erected since Maria.

Then he revisited the month before in Italy with only memories of Emma to keep him warm and realised he'd not been cold once since he'd returned to Australia, and it wasn't just the weather.

His new life had started with a funeral and ended with a rebirth. His. He remembered the first morning they'd woken together and the sound of the chimes he'd thought was the wind. The sight of that mystical bird's pure imitation of the stationary chimes had remained with him the whole time away. Along with Emma's face as she'd listened.

The whole of Lyrebird Lake had embraced him, the people, the land, the warmth, and all he needed from Emma was her acceptance of his right to be by her side and part of her children's lives. He swore to himself as he drove that he would make that happen.

When they stopped Emma woke and he said nothing as he waited for her to get her bearings. She sat up straighter and blinked. 'We're here?'

Her eyes looked bruised and he tightened his hands on the wheel to stop himself reaching for her. '*Si*, you slept.'

She looked around. The dark brick walls of

the hospice loomed over the courtyard where they'd parked and she couldn't help but wonder if this was where she'd end her days. That was beyond depressing when she looked at Gianni beside her. There was no way she'd allow Gianni to be with her then.

'Don't you have better things to do than visit my parents?' Emma had changed her mind about Gianni's presence at the hospice, a new urgency to keep him away from them, but he'd been persistently obstinate.

'At least let me meet the grandparents of my child.' He flashed a stern glance at her. 'You can't block me out of your life completely. And if you plan to exclude me, they should meet me so they will know of whom you speak.'

Emma sighed and gave in as she waited for Gianni to open her door.

A shaft of sunlight shone into the courtyard and fell on the blonde hair of Emma's mother, Clare. She sat strapped in a wheelchair with her husband by her side, and Emma dreaded the first few minutes of her visit every week because she never knew how her mother would be when she arrived.

Sometimes Clare was alert and almost focussed, other times morbidly depressed and railing against her condition.

The disease affected the way the brain worked and depression and anger had less controls left to keep them in check.

Once a beautiful woman, the ravages of the disease had screwed up Clare's face and twisted her body so that she seemed perched in the chair more than relaxed back in it.

Her blue eyes lit up when she saw Emma and her arm flung out in an uncontrolled greeting that almost knocked her husband's head. Her dad smiled and moved out of the way.

'So you know me today,' Emma said softly, and kissed her mother's cheek. She handed her father the roses she'd brought from home.

'Mum's roses are thriving. And I've brought a friend to see you both.'

Clare clapped her hands at the treat and Emma smiled. 'This is Gianni Bonmarito, from Italy. Gianni is filling in for Angus at the moment, and had to come up to Brisbane, so we came together.' She turned back to Gianni. 'This is my mother, Clare, and my father, Rex.'

Gianni lifted her mother's hand to his mouth and kissed it. Clare crowed loudly with delight and he smiled at her. 'It is true your daughter has your beautiful eyes.'

Then he shook hands with Rex. 'Sir.'

Rex didn't smile but his eyes softened. 'It's always nice to meet friends of Emma's. How long are you staying in Lyrebird Lake, Gianni?'

Gianni met his solid look. 'Only another week. Angus returns next Friday.'

Emma looked across and hoped her face was impassive. She could survive that long. In fact, the time had passed swiftly. That was a good thing.

His deep voice flowed around her as she thought about the realities of his departure, about the impact he'd had on her life, and the impact she wouldn't allow him. Then a change in his tone alerted her and his words sank in.

'There are many things I will miss about Queensland. But the hardest to leave will be Emma.' He stared straight into Rex's face. 'I come today because I wish to ask permission to court your daughter.'

Gianni heard the words come from his own mouth and wasn't sure who was most surprised—he or Emma. Or perhaps Rex?

Suddenly it was clear. It wasn't duty he was offering this woman—it was his heart. In his mind he still could see her calm face asleep in the car, trusting beside him, that feeling of rightness at keeping her safe.

That moment when she'd greeted her mother,

daughterly love searching for the recognition she'd found, had given him real joy. He'd been so glad for her because he loved Emma. He needed to be there for her as the Barbie doll's house that was her mother became emptier. He needed to be there for her if and when her brothers became ill, and when the time came, he wanted to be there when she opened the results for herself. Not because his life was forever tied to hers—or that the result affected his own unborn child—but to be her rock like Rex was the rock for Clare.

Emma's mouth dropped open. How dared he say that in front of her parents? With no warning? Make them think there was something between them?

Well, wasn't there? a sensible voice inside argued logically. A growing child she refused to discuss with him?

Emma gasped. She couldn't help her protest. 'You have no right to say that here, Gianni.'

Emma could feel the heat in her cheeks at her father's searching look. And Clare clapped her hands with childlike excitement. What had he been thinking to say that?

Gianni slanted a glance at her. 'It is customary to ask permission from your father.'

She shook her head at her parents as she tried to undo the damage Gianni had caused, but didn't know how. 'But not necessary, as I've already said no.'

'*Si*. But I will not give up.' He looked at her parents. 'I wish to show Emma and Grace my beautiful country. I am a wealthy man who has fallen in love with your daughter. Do I have your permission to woo her?'

Fallen in love? How dared he lie to her parents? To her?

'It's up to Emma but I have no objections.' Rex grinned at his fuming daughter. 'You should think about it, Emma. It sounds like a fabulous idea, to visit, at least. You've never had a holiday.' Rex looked from one to the other as Gianni brushed off Emma‘s complaint. He was no fool. 'And a great opportunity for Grace to broaden her horizons.'

'Dad,' Emma sighed with exasperation, 'it's not happening.'

The rest of the visit passed in a blur for Emma. She fumed and glared and cut short the visit so she could get him in the car and let him know what she thought of his underhand tactics. How dared he?

'I can't believe you said that. In front of my mother, as well. There is no way I would have taken you if I'd known you were going to do that.'

He nodded his head. 'So I believed.'

Emma threw her hands out in frustration. 'Don't you listen? I'm not marrying you. I'm not marrying anyone. You saw my mother. You saw my father.' She pointed her finger at him. 'I don't want a man tied to me like that.'

'Calm yourself, *cara*. I shared marriage with a woman who lived a month into my marriage. And have spent the last ten years regretting I didn't have more time with her. Are you so certain you have so much life to waste that you can disregard what you have the chance of now?'

That wasn't fair. 'My life is not a waste. I live each day as much as I can.' She tried every day to appreciate each new experience. 'I'm more aware how precious my day is than a lot of people. I guess I can thank the disease for that. But the question is, Gianni, do you have the rest of your life to waste with me?' Her head was spinning as she searched for arguments he would understand.

Gianni shook his head. 'My life has been a passage of time and my work. That I have wasted. It is only now that I am beginning to enjoy. Now you are here. So it would be a tragic waste if I missed the birth of our child, the progress of your pregnancy. I have decided I will not miss that.'

If only he knew. She wished she could have that too, she thought, but he went on.

He shrugged away the futility. 'It is too late to change that. I wish to spend my days and, of course, also the nights with you. The idea of you becoming ill in the future does not affect those wants and needs. Or my desire to be there for you.'

The notion was blissful but the reality unpalatable. 'I don't want a man tied to me like my father is tied to my mother.'

Gianni shook his head, denying her statement. 'Your father looked to be in the place he wanted to be and I admire him for that. He did not look tied. I liked your parents.' He paused to emphasise the next statement. 'Both of them.'

Emma blinked. He'd liked her parents. The concept made her pause. Had Gianni seen past what she sometimes forgot to look past? Her father was a wonderful man and it was true, he did not look like a victim. Her mother was ill, but cared for, and loved, and flashes of the woman who had been there for her when she'd been young could still be seen. Was it true that maybe she, Emma, had forgotten to look for them as much as she should, in her own fear for Grace?

Gianni went on. 'Of course you are scared of making a decision to tie yourself to a man you do not know well, and it is natural to worry if your health suffers. But you must remember, my circumstances give me the resources to deal with anything.' He lifted his brows. 'Wealth does not promise happiness but it is useful in certain circumstances. You are going to have to take a leap of faith too, and allow me into that part of your life.'

It sounded idyllic, but idealism wasn't reality. No. Never. Before yesterday she had to admit she'd been tempted. But the spectre of tomorrow had shown her she couldn't. 'I can't do that, Gianni.' Emma glanced out the front of the car and realised that they'd pulled up outside the headquarters of Huntington's Queensland.

They'd driven through the city already. Her meeting started in ten minutes. Inside were people with the same dilemmas she had. But braver people than her.

'Think about it, *cara*.' He glanced at his watch. 'I will be back by six and we can discuss this at dinner. I will come to your room at seven.'

She wouldn't let him wear her down. He'd done a bad thing by involving her parents. 'I won't be there. I'll stay somewhere else. I don't trust you.'

He didn't seem surprised by her outburst. 'That is foolish. You cannot deny we need to talk and time is running out. In a week I must leave to complete what I have committed to. Stay for tonight. I have already booked the rooms.'

* * *

Emma didn't move out of the five-star hotel. She told herself it was because she hated waste and the room was to die for—and material comfort would substitute for another kind.

Fifteen-foot-high ceilings, velvet drapes from floor to ceiling, the deep blush of rosewood furnishings, a bath she could have floated a canoe in.

She stared at the ornate ceiling as she soaked. Even in the bathroom they had sculpted cornices. She thought about a man who wanted to marry her and be the father to her children. Who'd lied to her parents and said he loved her.

There was the strong chance he would shower her and her daughter with gifts, show them both the world, and continue to state that he loved her.

All strange things to complain of, and not the only dilemmas. She prided herself on her independence but how independent was she really going to be when the new baby was born?

It was a long way off, an embryo barely the size of a peanut, but there none the less. In seven months time he or she would certainly have an impact on her work and her finances and her ability to support herself.

And what if she wasn't positive for the gene? Was she throwing away her one chance at love? Because though Gianni didn't really love her, she did love him. She had realised that as she'd driven away from Grace. Was she wasting something precious, as Gianni said? She couldn't deny that Gianni touched her on a level no man had ever come near to. She could feel his presence, felt complete when he was around, and he had rights too, rights to share his child. But she couldn't and wouldn't marry him if she was positive for the gene. It had been her whole focus in her life to prepare for the end as a single woman. She needed to keep her distance until after the result.

* * *

Dinner undid all her resolutions.

Gianni in a black tie made her mouth dry and her chest hurt. Since arriving at the hotel, one he apparently had stayed at before because every person knew his name and couldn't do enough for him, he'd changed.

He'd slipped into another, grander persona that blew her resistance to smithereens.

He emanated effortless command, far too much power and tightly leashed control for one man, and on their arrival in the restaurant she could see that the maître d' agreed that Gianni deserved special treatment.

The table was discreet, service invisible but incredibly efficient. The chef dropped by to ensure the meal was adequate and the wine tasted like ambrosia. She'd thought the Lakehouse amazing but this was on another level.

'You've changed.' And she hadn't. Reality check.

He shrugged. Totally at ease in his persona.

'No. This is me.' He gestured to the room. 'At work I change.'

She frowned and the uncomfortable thought of extreme wealth perturbed her. 'Just how well off are you?'

He raised one sardonic eyebrow in that autocratic way he sometimes affected that annoyed her. 'Are you really interested?'

Despite her irritation she thought about it. Like the time he'd asked if she was interested in cars. In the big picture it really was the least of her worries. She almost laughed. 'Not really.'

His lips twitched and that tiny touch of amusement shared made her belly warm. 'I didn't think so. But it is reasonable that you should know there is this side of me, as well.'

She looked at him. Looked like she remembered doing once before, and had to admit he was pretty spectacular. The black suit had a dull silk gleam that spared no detail of his magnificent physique. How could she sit opposite this man and ignore him when he blatantly told the world he was her man? That her wish was his command? That only the best was good enough for her? She had no idea but she'd try, and if she didn't succeed she could tell herself she'd done her best.

The meal passed in a blur—entrée, main course, dessert, half-finished plates removed—and suddenly the tragedy of it all overwhelmed her. It wasn't fair. She wanted him to look at her like he was looking now for the rest of her life. She ached to make plans and discuss her pregnancy and have someone she could share the highs and lows of life and parenthood, even her work, with, and Gianni could be that person. Was offering that dream, but there was a chance that after tomorrow she couldn't accept it.

It was tearing her apart and she bowed under the pressure of what was coming.

And then Gianni touched her. He must have seen the change in her expression.

He cupped her cheek in a caress that came from across the table but emptied the room of people and furniture and noise until she seemed to be suspended in the air, his hand on her cheek, floating in space, just the two of them. How did he do that?

When he took his hand away and she landed, mentally, back on her chair in a crowded restaurant, it was just as powerful a demonstration.

She dragged her eyes away, clawing for composure, until he captured her knee between his under the long tablecloth, deliberately, cleaving her back to him effortlessly.

These tables were two darned tiny for someone fighting to keep their head above water, she complained in her mind, but the complaint was overwritten by the heat and raw need she could feel bubbling up between them.

'Bill, please,' he said quietly, and the waiter appeared as if it was his sole aim in life to be there when Gianni called.

Bill, please, her foggy brain echoed. It all seemed to be happening in a cloud now and that was without alcohol. The waiter had been and gone, and Gianni's eyes were back on hers and she watched him stand. Felt him move behind her and she half stood as he pulled the chair out and dropped her wrap across her shoulders, along with his arm.

They moved to the elevator bank across from the restaurant and suddenly she was fiercely jealous of her space with Gianni. She glanced around and 'their' elevator arrived, and she wanted to be in there with the door shut before anyone else intruded on the intimate space around them. She had no idea how she'd come to that frame of mind but she was locked into his gravity like his personal moon.

She even sighed with relief when the door shut and they were alone.

'I'd hoped we'd have the elevator to ourselves,' he murmured, and his arm tightened as she turned to face him fully, and his eyes burned into hers as he kissed her. Somehow his back was against the rear wall and she was returning his kiss like there was no tomorrow.

With Gianni's mouth firm and hot against her own, it was impossible not to lose herself in the taste and texture of this long-awaited homecoming. But the doors opened and he put her from him with a small smile.

'I think we need somewhere a little more private than this,' he murmured into her ear, and held his hand over the door edge while she dithered confusedly with her scattered wits and almost stumbled from the elevator. There was no time for tangos tonight.

Gianni watched Emma wake for the second time in his life and wanted to lock the door and never let her leave. It seemed she would have him, he thought with satisfaction. He felt his cultural heritage very strongly this morning. *Amore.*

'*Buongiorno*, Emma, *dolce.* Or good morning,

sweet Emma,' he said as he sat down beside her on the bed.

Emma blinked and sat up. He saw her look around and realise they had succumbed again. Judging by the way she inhaled the unmistakable aroma of fresh espresso, she was rapidly becoming grounded.

'Un caffe?'

She didn't quite meet his eyes. 'I gather that means coffee, and, yes, please.'

He liked the way she didn't clutch the bed sheet as tightly to her neck after all that had passed between them last night but lifted it over her breasts and tucked it loosely behind her back.

'Did you sleep well?' she asked with that hint of shyness that told him she was pretending to be relaxed. He handed her a cup. Sweet Emma.

'Eventually, like the dead.' He smiled wickedly at her. 'And you?' Her cheeks dusted a delightfully rosy pink and he wanted to take the cup from her and see where the blush ended, but she was sitting there sipping the coffee with her elbows tucked into her sides as a safeguard from the sheet slipping.

She didn't look very comfortable, he thought with a wry smile.

'Heavily enough not to hear breakfast arrive.' Her eyes skittered away and he saw where her thoughts led. He hastened to reassure her.

'I took the tray at the door and you looked beautiful as you dreamt. I think your dreams were pleasant.'

'So I had a silly smile on my face, did I?' More embarrassment, and this time he did take the cup and put it down on the bedside table.

'Not silly. My dreams were sweet also.' He drew her into his arms. 'Thank you for my sweet dreams, Emma.'

He ran the tip of his finger slowly down her shoulder and marvelled at the sensation. 'Your skin is like silk, so soft and beautiful. Everything about you makes me aware of the beauty in this world. Things I haven't seen for years, like the sunrise this morning while you slept, the moon last night shining off your skin so that you glowed like a lustrous pearl, even the lights of the city were all more beautiful because I share this time with you.'

His mouth brushed hers and then settled against her, and Emma's eyes drifted shut as she savoured the taste of coffee and Gianni and the feel of his arms around her. She never wanted it to end but that time was drawing near. More quickly than she expected when his phone rang and they broke apart.

He frowned down at the instrument as it lay on the bedside table and finally he picked it up. By which time Emma was firmly grounded. And pleased to have the moment to regather her wits.

'*Scusi*,' he said, and rose to stand at the window. Emma slipped from the bed, dragging the sheet, and took the moment to escape to the bathroom.

She caught a glimpse of her cheeks in the mirror, rosy pink like her slightly swollen lips, and she toyed again with the idea that he truly did find her necessary for his happiness.

Some time during the night when he had been sleeping beside her, she too had seen the moon and it had dusted the harsh lines of his face with a softness that had clutched at her heart. She'd wished she could say yes to his proposal and all he promised her; she even considered the idea that if the results came back as she expected, if she was positive, then she could call it off. Just so she could pretend she could be Gianni's wife for an hour or two to see how it felt.

But it wouldn't be fair. Or sensible, and she couldn't guarantee he wouldn't guess what she intended.

She bundled the sheet up, placed it on the bathroom stool and slipped into the huge shower. The hot water cascaded over her shoulders and she closed her eyes. Her body ached, she was a little stiff and tender and intimate moments she'd shared with Gianni came back to her in erotic, blushing detail as she stood there and soaped her breasts and belly.

It had come to the end. Finished, because today was the day. Every day she'd counted down to the end of not knowing. To having no choice but to accept her fate. The fate of Grace. The fate of their unknown baby. And by proxy the fate of her love for Gianni. Suddenly she didn't want him to see her in the shower.

No matter that they'd spent a delightful episode there during the night; this morning was a new, momentous day and she needed to create distance before she caved in and told him what was happening. Hastily she turned off the water and dried herself in a huge towel before slipping on the thick white robe that hung behind the door.

When she opened the bathroom door she found the maid had been. How had he achieved that so quickly? But the bed was fresh and turned down, in case…what?

With breakfast laid out on the table on the spacious veranda overlooking the Brisbane River, Gianni finished his phone conversation when she reappeared.

'Bonguiorno.' The warmth in his eyes did strange things to her already slightly nauseated stomach but she decided that breakfast was a necessity, given the day she was going to have.

'Good morning again, Gianni.' Then she clarified her day so there could be no confusion. 'I have an appointment at noon and afterwards I'll visit my parents again, but I'd like to go on my own.' She looked up. 'My plans should take an hour or two after lunch. Is it acceptable for you to leave for Lyrebird Lake after that?'

He tilted her head, unable to miss the change in her. 'You are very businesslike after your shower, Emma.'

She avoided his eyes. 'I have a big day ahead.'

'Anything you'd like to discuss?' He was watching her. Sensing her evasion.

She picked up her coffee cup and took a sip of the warm liquid and grimaced at the strong taste. 'No. Thank you.'

'Then eat. I will shower.' He glanced around for his watch and picked it up. 'Perhaps I could drop you off at your appointment.'

She shook her head. 'I'd rather you didn't. I'll catch a taxi.'

He frowned but finally nodded. 'You may leave your things here as I have taken the room for the rest of the day for a meeting after lunch.'

'It makes it easier if I know I'm not holding you up. So it would work if I saw you back here this afternoon.'

He shrugged at her stubbornness. 'As you wish. I will arrange a taxi when you're ready to leave.'

CHAPTER NINE

THE taxi pulled up outside the glass-and-steel building in the middle of Brisbane. She wondered, not for the first time, why a building you would associate with life-changing events should look so ordinary. For Emma it was as if it hid the secrets of the world behind those blank windows that soared up to the sky.

It had been easier than she'd thought to shake Gianni, and she squashed the traitorous thoughts that wondered if perhaps it would have been better if she hadn't. Of course she should do this on her own. It was something she'd tried not to imagine doing and there was an almost strange relief that after today she wouldn't have to dread it again. What would be would be.

'Sit down, Emma. Nice to see you again.' Jenny Bloom was a thin-faced brunette with a severe bob and the warmest brown eyes Emma had ever seen.

'Hi, Jenny.' Emma settled herself and discreetly inhaled an extra-big breath to settle her nerves.

'Didn't bring anyone?'

'No. I wanted some time to myself to think about it.'

Jenny nodded. 'Fair enough.' She shuffled some papers on her desk, withdrew an envelope and then stood up. 'Would you like me to leave while you read that?' She reached over and offered the envelope to Emma.

Emma's heart seemed to be thumping in her ears, not her chest, and she automatically took the envelope, though gingerly, as if it were a time bomb. In a way it was.

A letter bomb that could hold her and her daughter's, and now her and Gianni's future. She should have brought him. The realisation that this was one hundred per cent Gianni's business arrowed uncomfortably into her heaving emotions. But it was too late now.

She looked at Jenny. 'Do you know what's in there?'

If anything, Jenny's eyes grew warmer. 'Yes. I do.'

Emma couldn't tell anything from the counsellor's face and she guessed she'd had plenty of practice at poker. 'Then how about you tell me?'

Jenny nodded and sat down. 'The results came in on Friday, as I said.' She paused and stared straight at Emma. 'As you know, the laboratory analysis comes in two cag repeat numbers. Your mother's numbers were a seventeen and a forty-four. Therefore she did have the HD gene as forty-four is above the thirty-six cut-off for inevitable disease process.' Without more ado, she went on, 'Your numbers are 17 and 17, which means you and your children are not at risk of having the Huntington's gene.'

Sudden nausea came out of nowhere. Emma clamped her lips shut and inhaled desperately through her nostrils. Slowly her head cleared and her stomach settled. But she still didn't know what to think. The expected bloom of relief, the explosion of joy that she was safe from the gene, as were Grace and the baby, the incredible dropping of an enormous weight, didn't come.

All she could do was stretch her face into a caricature of a smile and offer it to Jenny. What she felt was a grey wall of sadness that seemed to sink over her. She, out of all her family, would be free of the spectre yet more tied to it than any of the others by watching and worrying for them. She felt like a survivor from the *Titanic*.

She'd never felt so alone in her life and Emma ached to have Gianni beside her. Her hand in his. Drawing on his strength, which she knew he would have offered. She realised Jenny was speaking but no sound could penetrate her isolation yet. Slowly the world returned and she hoped relief would come later.

'It's okay, Emma.' Jenny watched her with compassion and no judgement. 'You don't have to be thrilled and it's natural to think of your family. Are you sure there's no one I can call?'

She almost said it. Almost asked for him—but then remembered he had a business meeting. Where would she start in explaining why she hadn't asked him to come? How would she tell him she'd been? She closed her eyes and tried to think what she would have done if there had been no Gianni. Incredible how hard that was. Her mind cleared.

'I'll go and see Mum and Dad.' She looked around the office and surprisingly it still looked the same. Nothing momentous had happened in the room, so nothing had changed. Something momentous had only happened to her.

Late that afternoon, when Gianni saw Emma enter the suite, he knew something had occurred. Something large in her life. Something she had excluded him from.

His first thought was the baby but she had no signs that her issues were physical. The emotional stress was plain to see and his stomach sank at the reality of his own guilt. His fault. He'd done this.

It must be that again she regretted their night together, and because he had grown to love her he began to wonder if it would be better for him to leave. For good. Of all things, he wanted Emma to be happy.

'Does the fact that we spent the night together make you feel so bad that you cannot be happy, Emma? What can I do to replace the smile on your face?'

'I need my space, Gianni. I have a lot on my mind and I can't think when I am with you.'

'I can see you are burdened. Why can't you share those burdens with me?'

She shook her head. 'That's not how I do it.'

His eyes narrowed with exasperation. 'Perhaps you should learn. For both of us. For our unborn child.'

She sighed so heavily he wanted to lay her head against his chest. Why would she not let him in? 'Our child is the one dilemma I can't see my way past.'

'Then let me worry for you.' He sat her down on the lounge and took her hand in his. The words came heavily and his heart ached because it seemed she could never be happy with him. Perhaps if he left her to think, things would change, but he wasn't sure any more. He squeezed her hand. It was the best he could do for the moment.

He looked down at her. 'So tell me what happened in Brisbane that changed you.'

Emma didn't want to. Didn't want to face this

moment and admit the doubts and the lack of faith in Gianni she'd had. Now she could see her fears were unfounded but her own confusion had masked that. Until too late. Too late to change the way she'd planned her day.

But it was the time to be brave. She'd lied to him by omission this morning. She wouldn't lie to him again.

'Today I picked up the results from my genetic testing.'

He didn't say anything so she stumbled on. Saying it quickly and for the first time out loud. 'I don't have the gene.'

His face was expressionless. Too expressionless. 'You found this out today?'

His response wasn't what she expected. It was almost as if the results were unimportant.

She said it again. For both of them. 'I don't have the genetic predisposition for Huntington's disease.'

'Of course it is good you are free of that worry.'

He brushed that off. 'But you went for these results on your own? While I was this close to you?' His black brows snapped together, and she tightened her hold on his hand in case he pulled away.

Her voice faltered. 'Afterwards, I thought about how it would have been nice to have you there.'

'Nice?' He shook his head as he assimilated her choice to exclude him. 'Nice to be present when the fate of the woman I love and my child is decided?'

He didn't love her. He was just saying that. He shook his head again and her stomach sank at the degree of his distress. 'I agree,' he said coldly. 'I do believe it would have been—' the sarcasm thickened '—*nice* to be there, myself.'

He looked down at her and she shivered at the bleakness in his eyes. He peeled her fingers away. Untangled them one by one as if they offended him. 'You really don't need me at all, do you, Emma? You want to be your own person. Alone with Grace. With your own decisions, no matter if they are wrong or right.'

'I should have asked you to come.'

'You forget, I have told you of my love for you. I do not have the luxury of turning that emotion off.' His eyes lingered on her face and he shook his head. 'Like you seem to be able to do.'

Then he said the words that sent a coldness along her spine that she doubted would ever go. 'I will leave next week and not bother you. But I must have access to my child, must have news of your pregnancy, and of course financially I will support you in whatever you need.'

He was leaving. She'd achieved what she'd thought she'd wanted. Well, if he left, he wasn't paying her for having his child. It was her child, too.

She had her pride. 'I don't want your money. That won't be necessary.'

He stood up and looked down at her. 'For me it

is. You have no choice. You are not giving me an inch, Emma. This I will not be swayed from.'

It was all too much. She couldn't take much more before she dissolved into a weeping frenzy that once started she doubted she'd be able to stop. Would this day never end?

She couldn't take any more, and mostly because she knew she was at fault. 'As you wish,' she said, and stumbled into the bathroom to hide her face.

CHAPTER TEN

WHEN they picked up Grace after a silent trip back from Brisbane, Emma alighted quickly and knelt to scoop up her daughter in her arms.

She hugged Grace with a fierceness that made Gianni's chest hurt with all that he had lost. After a minute Grace wriggled free as if overwhelmed by the unexpected fervour of her mother's embrace, and he saw Emma's flinch of distress.

He understood her anguish. It was what she had done to him.

Even though he was not a part of her life, that Grace was free of the spectre that had haunted Emma was a reason to smile, if a trifle grimly, at his own exclusion.

'Hello, Grace.' He got out of the car to take

her little suitcase. When he bent down to shake her hand she leaned forward and unexpectedly kissed both his cheeks in the Continental fashion. Diverted, Gianni smiled. 'And who has been teaching you Italian customs?'

'Nana and I watched a movie and there were Italian people in it. That's what the people did when they met. I asked and Nana said that was how people greeted each other in your country.'

'That is true. I thank you.' He had tilted Emma's seat forward so the little girl could slip past it. Once in the vehicle, she bounced around like a little cricket in the back until her mother told her to put her seat belt on. The old Gianni would have winced at the risk to fine leather—the new one smiled with amusement.

'I've never been in a sports car before,' Grace chattered as Emma seated herself again and Gianni shut her door. He could hear her ask if the car went fast but he didn't hear Emma's answer. He could have told her it did.

When he climbed back in behind the wheel, Grace asked where Gianni's house was because apparently her grandmother had shown her a map of Italy.

'In the outskirts of Portofino, what was once a small Italian fishing village. Now it is also a tourist resort in the province of Genoa on the Italian Riviera. I have a beautiful home.' He paused and glanced at Emma. 'I had hoped to take you and your mother there one day.'

The glance he received from Emma would have stripped paint off the inside of his hire car but he was over guarding her sensibilities. It was the truth. And she was the one who prevented such a thing. When he glanced in the rear-vision mirror he could see that Grace thought it was a fine idea.

'I'd like to see Portofino,' Grace piped up, and

after a pause she looked at her mother's stiff neck and subsided.

Emma didn't speak once on the short ride home but Grace made up for it. Even in the heavy mood of the car, mostly caused by Emma's silence, Gianni found it a novelty to listen to the chatter of an excited child as she discussed the circus and her visit.

'Thank you for the lift,' Emma said stiffly when they pulled up at her house. She didn't wait for him to open her door and Gianni narrowed his eyes at her. What had happened in Brisbane would lie between them until it was discussed again because the change in their rapport had been catastrophic. But this time he would not be the one who chased her. And time was running out.

By the time he was out of the car she had extricated Grace from her seat belt and bustled her up the path to the house without a backward glance. Grace turned and waved, and he waved back.

Emma's coldness left a knot in his chest that made him frown. He closed her door thoughtfully and returned to his car.

The next afternoon, after work, Emma dragged her feet up the path and under the rose arch to her front door. When she was inside she sank back against the panels and kicked off her shoes. In stockinged feet she trailed across to the kitchen window and gazed out. She had done so many absent-minded things today that if she hadn't had the results she'd be sure she was coming down with her mother's disease.

She'd avoided Gianni too successfully and began to doubt if she could continue for another four days. Even though Angus and Mia returned on Friday and then he'd be gone for ever.

The greyness she'd caught like a virus after the results and the resulting emotional battle with Gianni had sapped her strength and all she wanted to do was sit on the veranda and gaze out over the lake to find some peace.

She stripped off her stockings and filled a glass with water before she wandered towards the back door. Such was her state of mind she even left the water by the sink.

No flutter of apprehension in her belly warned her. No prickling of hairs on her neck and certainly no noise. Emma's mind remained totally focussed on the decision she'd made last night. And with Grace not due home for fifteen minutes she could allow herself to be as miserable as she liked for a few brief minutes.

She pushed open the old screen door onto the veranda. The soft sole of her foot lifted, exposed and unprotected, when instead of the hard wood of the veranda as she'd felt a million times before she felt the sinuous circular thickness of something that contracted under her instep and then the sudden sharp pinpricks of fire as the snake struck.

The four-foot reptile arched its head and struck again as she stumbled backwards into the house and the last things she saw was the flicker of crimson under the black belly as the snake's tail disappeared off the veranda and into the bushes.

Red-belly, she thought still with icy-cold horror and a mounting flare of panic, but there was just a glimmer of relief. It wasn't the deadly poisonous and vicious brown snake there'd been sightings of lately. Thank God, and thanks also that it had been her and not Grace that had been struck.

Her brain, mashed from shock, stared unseeingly at where the snake had disappeared. On one leg she twisted to stare at the twin bite marks on her heel and ankle. The pain was building and she needed to bind her leg and stop movement. Movement would pump the poison around her body. Around her baby.

That fear clutched at her heart.

Emma blinked away stinging tears and reached for her mobile in her pocket but discovered she'd left it at work when she'd turned it off that morning. More brain mush.

All she could think was she wanted Gianni but her mind couldn't process a plan of action.

She couldn't stay standing there and she needed a bandage. Her head felt funny but it was probably the shock of the bite. She lowered herself carefully onto the floor and stretched her leg out in front of her.

She needed a bandage. With a snakebite victim you were supposed to bandage from the bite down and then up again and then down again. Enough to compress but not enough to occlude blood flow. And not move. That was all she could remember. But how did you get the bandage if you weren't allowed to move?

The pain shot in tendrils of acid-like burning up her ankle and she wiped her forehead with the back of her hand as the sweat trickled into her eyes. Nausea hovered and she glanced around for something in case she was sick. How on earth did one throw up without moving? she thought mistily.

All these years she'd worried about the onset of Huntington's and here she was almost dying from a snakebite, though people didn't usually die from black snakes, unless they frightened themselves to death, and she could see the danger of that.

Her heart beat at her ribs like a caged bird trying to escape, and she forced herself to slow her breathing into some semblance of control.

Black snakes didn't usually attack unless provoked and she guessed she must have upset it when she'd stood on it. But she'd never had one at the door before. What if it had been a King brown? She'd be pushing up daisies before she knew it.

She tried not to think about poison soaking into her blood like ink into chalk. She looked around at the kitchen. She had a strange perspective from sitting on the floor and decided it was what infants saw when they crawled around.

She wouldn't have minded a sip of that water she'd left by the sink but the cupboards seemed to loom away from her and she wasn't game to move. It was scary sitting here on the floor by herself. And uncomfortable. And lonely.

Was this what her life was always going to be like in moments of crisis because she'd locked everyone else out? She knew she didn't like it. The lonely interim while she waited for the end that would come in some form—though not as she'd imagined it the last eight years. She could see she'd concentrated on the destination of her life more than the journey but was it something she could change now that she knew her destiny did not lie with the Huntington's gene? It was certainly something Gianni wanted her to change. She could have had a lovely affair with Gianni after all. Maybe even a lovely marriage. Silly fool.

The front door opened and she heard Grace's step.

Thank goodness. 'Down here, darling.'

Grace dropped her satchel beside Emma and knelt down. 'Why're you on the floor?'

Emma looked again at her heel and ankle and licked impossibly dry lips. 'A snake bit me.'

Grace's eyes widened and then screwed up in fright. 'What type?'

Emma reached out her hand and gripped Grace's arm. 'It's okay. A red-belly.'

Grace's head swivelled. 'Where?'

Emma pointed to her foot. 'On my ankle.' Grace shook her head and kept scanning the room and Emma understood the question this time. 'On the veranda. It's gone now.'

Grace sighed with relief and then looked quickly at her mother. 'Are you going to be all right?' She didn't wait for an answer as she stood up straight. 'I'll get Gianni.'

How strange her daughter thought of Gianni

first, too. And not Andy or Ben or her other grandfather. 'I have his mobile number in my bag if you'll bring it.'

Grace was back before she'd almost finished speaking. Emma stroked her arm. 'It's okay. Good girl. I'll be fine.'

She rummaged in her bag but couldn't find the number. She knew it was there. Her head swam but shock and the nausea she'd had all day more than accounted for it. The paper crackled and she pulled it out and Grace snatched it and ran for the phone in the bedroom.

Gianni was about to leave work when his phone rang. He flipped it open with unusual impatience. He wanted to see Emma.

'Gianni?' A little girl's voice. 'It's Grace.'

His heart rate picked up at the fear in her voice. 'Grace? What's wrong?'

'Mummy's been bitten by a red-belly snake.'

It felt as though a boxer had stepped up to him and hit him as hard as he could in the centre of his chest. Then his heart started again. A snake. Not again. His worst nightmare and a vicious irony.

He swallowed and cleared his throat. 'Grace. Where is she?'

Grace sniffed and he could tell she was trying to hold back tears. 'Just inside the back door. At home.'

'Hang on, little one. I'm on my way.' He looked up at Christine, who would share the evening shift with Andy. 'I'm bringing Emma in, she's been bitten by a red-and-black snake. Your Australian snakes. How bad are they?'

'Red-belly black snake.' Christine rummaged in the emergency kit. 'Not usually too bad for adults. Go bring her in.'

Gianni brought the bandages Christine had thrust into his hands. He came through the house at speed, with Grace glued to his back after she'd opened the door for him. Emma sat and smiled tiredly when she saw him. Emma was alive and conscious and his breath eased out.

To Emma he was the most beautiful sight in the world.

'Hello there, little Emma,' he said, and crouched down beside her. Her eyes widened to drink in the sight of him. He whistled silently when he saw the twin spots of blood and the gradual redness that was surrounding the bites.

'Nasty.' He slid the bandage out of its pack and began to bandage her ankle, down her foot and back up again. 'We'll do this and then I'll take you in. I still think I can get you to hospital quicker than the ambulance will get here.'

She winced as he bandaged over the area and his hands paused and then gentled before he continued. 'Sorry.'

She moistened her lips. 'I trod on it. Accidentally.'

He continued his bandaging. 'So that's why it bit you.'

She nodded. 'Twice, I think, and then it shot away.'

'Christine says they'll have a snake venom detection kit ready, but asked if you're still sure it was red underneath.'

'Yes.' She touched his arm. She could see he was pale with fear for her. 'It's not the worst snake and it might not have injected much poison.'

He nodded grimly. 'Not like the brown apparently, who loves to dump as much into your bloodstream as possible. I hate snakes. I'll be pleased when we get confirmation you are safe.' He looked over his shoulder at Grace and lowered his voice. 'You are both safe.' Then he scrutinised her face. 'You're looking pale and sweaty.'

She breathed out heavily. 'I feel sick. It was all

so quick.' She too glanced at Grace. 'And I'm scared, too.''

'I feel sick and I wasn't bitten.' He smiled grimly at her. 'I'd rather it had bitten me than you.'

He was serious, she realised. 'Me, too. But you've had enough bad luck with them.'

'An understatement. Now you sound more like yourself.' He finished bandaging and tucked the end in. 'Right, then.' He reached down and lifted her off the floor as if she were as light as one of Louisa's scones. When he was upright she was in his arms against his chest.

They should have got the ambulance. 'Your back. I'm heavy!'

'Spoken like a true nurse.' He smiled and turned to see that Grace was behind them. 'Come along, Grace, we'll take Mummy to the hospital, but we'll use her car. Can you find her keys, please?'

Grace opened the screen door at the front and

closed the main door after them as she followed. She rummaged in Emma's bag as she walked.

'I've been wanting to carry your mother like this for a while,' he said over his shoulder. 'It's a shame we have to go to the hospital.'

'Why do men like women to be helpless?' Emma couldn't help the tinge of sarcasm in her voice but she was beginning to see why women liked it. Incredible how much better she felt already with Gianni's arms around her.

She closed her eyes, wishing the world wasn't swirling because it interfered with her enjoyment of something that had never happened to her before. Her cheek rested against his shirt and she could hear his heart beat reassuringly in her ear as they crossed the veranda and went down the steps. She rubbed her cheek back and forth on his shirt and it was pleasantly scratchy against her skin. The feeling dulled the ache in her leg for a few moments and must be a good thing if it took her mind off the horror that the venom might affect their baby. 'Promise me you'll do this for me one day when I don't feel sick.'

'My pleasure.' She didn't need to open her eyes to know he was smiling. Her angle in his arms shifted as he reached one hand down to open the rear door of her car. 'You'll be better with your feet up so we'll take your car. You can sit in the front, Grace.' He turned and manoeuvred Emma in and reluctantly she let go of his neck and slid obediently backwards across the rear seat. 'We'll be there in a minute,' he said, and dropped a light kiss on her forehead.

She nodded and dragged a breath in through her nose to keep the nausea at bay. When she opened her eyes again they were there and Christine had a stretcher ready for her and Andy and Montana hovered with concern in their eyes.

The snake-venom detection kit was waiting and Christine snipped an area in the bandage to expose the bite areas. 'Looks like he got you twice,' she said as she dampened a cotton bud and wiped the spots to capture the venom left on the surface.

'Well, I did land on his back,' Emma sighed, and rested her head back and closed her eyes. The world swam so she opened them hurriedly again and watched Christine. She undid the yellow tube and swished the swab around in the dilutant then replaced the lid to invert the little tube several times.

Gianni touched her shoulder. 'I need to insert a cannula into your arm, Emma, in case you need medication. I'll run some fluids, as well.' He brushed the hair off her forehead. 'You're still too pale and interesting for me.'

'I'm always interesting,' she murmured with only a hint of her former fire, and Gianni squeezed her fingers before he began his preparations.

By the time the ten minutes of waiting to see which snake had bitten her was up, Gianni had the cannula in, her arm strapped and some saline running into her veins.

'Positive for black-snake venom.' Christine held the little strip of veils against the test legend. 'And also tiger snake, but you always take the first positive well first—so that proves who your ex-friend was.'

'Ex-friend is right, and I'd say he was just as scared as I was.' Emma's shoulders eased a little with the confirmation.

Gianni handed over the blood he'd taken from Emma when he'd inserted the line, and Christine began to test that for evidence of venom in Emma's blood. The answer to that would determine if she needed anti-venom or not. She doubted she would because after her initial panic she was calming down.

It took ten minutes but that answer was worth waiting for. 'No venom in her bloodstream on this test,' Christine said with a wobble in her voice that communicated to all how worried she'd been.

Gianni's breath huffed out and Emma's eyes met his. Their baby should be fine. 'How is your pain?' Gianni lifted her hand and felt her pulse, which seemed silly when she was connected to monitors.

'The machine's over there, Gianni.' She pointed with a teasing smile. 'And it tells you my pulse, and my blood pressure and oxygen saturation.'

'Stop your complaining,' he said, and continued to feel her wrist, but now a smile was on his lips, as well. Emma decided she couldn't have enough hand holding today and Gianni's seemed to work better than everyone else's.

She glanced at the monitor herself. 'My pulse is still higher than normal.'

'Of course. I am holding your hand.' Gianni raised his eyebrows. 'Then again, mine is almost double what it should be, and I did not annoy a snake.'

That was twice he'd said that. She realised there was less colour in his face, as well. 'Did I frighten you very badly, Gianni?'

'Frighten?' He shook his head. 'No.' He grimaced. 'You scared the life out of me, but we will talk of that later when I am sure you do not need anti-venom. Two results are not enough for me.' He glanced again at the monitor. 'Your vital signs are stable. Enough for me to almost believe the snake did not inject much venom into you. You have no symptoms of palpitations or breathlessness and your nausea is no worse.' He seemed to be reassuring himself more than her.

Emma lifted her other hand, despite the encumbrances of the intravenous infusion, and laid it over his. 'Black snakes might sink their fangs in if they get frightened but they don't often try to inject much venom unless they're really trapped,' Emma said, and she squeezed his wrist. 'Actually, the nausea's fading.'

'So is mine,' Gianni said. They smiled at each other. 'I'll leave so you can give Christine a specimen of urine and we'll check that as well as your blood again for circulating venom.'

Gianni left the room and peripherally he saw that the rest of the ward was still busy. He really didn't care. He'd leave that to Andy.

He needed a moment to comprehend the absolute horror of his future had Emma been bitten by a more deadly snake. He, more than anyone, knew what a venomous reptile could do. And it had not been pretty.

It had brought home the savagery of nature's pecking order and the ramifications of that event from ten years ago had certainly coloured his experience today. He couldn't imagine how he'd be feeling now if another woman he loved had been fighting for her life.

Even the thought of that scenario made sweat dampen the hairs on his arms and increase his heart rate. It seemed he had better do something to make sure he kept Emma a lot closer to him than he had been. Enough of these games. He was going nowhere unless she was with him. She would be glued to his side and he would not take no for an answer.

CHAPTER ELEVEN

'SO YOU can go home.' Andy said. As the emergency doctor on for the evening, it was up to him, not Gianni, when Emma could go.

'Almost an anticlimax,' Emma said, not meeting Gianni's eyes. He'd been amazing all afternoon but there was an implacable determination in his face that spoke of unfinished business. And she thought perhaps she was ready to hear it.

Andy explained their agreement on the findings, that the snake had bitten but not injected enough poison to affect her body systemically, and therefore that of her baby. But they would keep a close eye on her. 'You'll probably still get some swelling in your glands and perhaps a little discomfort up your leg. Rest up.' He glanced at

Gianni with raised eyebrows. 'Are you looking after her tonight?'

'She will keep her leg elevated, and Grace and I will wait on her this afternoon.'

'More spaghetti Bol?' she teased. It felt good to be back exchanging banter with Gianni. She'd started to lose that lightness since she'd discovered her pregnancy and the final blow had come on Sunday with the shock of her results. But it was fizzing back with the realisation that the time had come to stop pretending she didn't want to love him. Together they would sort something out. That was what she hadn't considered.

'Montana asked if you wanted Grace to stay over with Dawn tonight,' Andy said straight-faced.

'Thank you.' Gianni answered for her, though he did look to see if she disagreed. 'But I think she should stay with us and be reassured her mother is safe.'

Emma felt the glow inside her expand. That

was her instinct too, and the unselfishness of Gianni's reaction was incredibly reassuring. He was right, perfectly right, for all of their sakes. How on earth could she not love him?

'Of course.' Andy didn't miss the byplay between them and his smile widened. 'She's welcome any time.'

Gianni nodded but his eyes were on Emma. He bent down and lifted her into his arms and her fingers slid around his neck. She couldn't not love him. She tightened her grip and he looked down at her, giving her a possessive hug. He was everything she wanted in a man and a snake had taught her that life was too short to risk happiness now.

'We will talk when I have you home,' he said softly so that only she could hear. He glanced at her daughter with a smile. 'Grace can discuss snake safety with her Barbies when the time comes.'

And so it happened. Grace played happily on

the floor in the kitchen with her doll's house and Emma sat on Gianni's lap with her legs up along the lounge. They held hands as they gazed out over the veranda rail. Gianni had checked assiduously that no unwanted guests were lurking before he would allow Emma or her daughter outside onto the wooden area.

'It was just bad luck,' Emma said as she looked down at their entwined fingers. 'And look what good came out of it.'

Gianni squeezed her hand. 'We would have arrived eventually but such a fright has hastened the course.'

'So what course has been hastened?' she teased, and he smiled down at her.

He sat back a little so he could see her face properly. 'So you are ready to listen to me now, are you?'

She bit her lip. 'I might be.'

'I do not accept "might" any more from you, *cara*. The time for hesitation is past.'

He lifted her off his lap and placed her gently back down again on the lounge. Then he took her hand and dropped to one knee.

Emma felt a blush rush up her neck and she tried to pull him up off his knees. 'No. Don't do that.'

He ignored her as he gazed up into her face. 'Even with snakes I would do this. And know I have never knelt before a woman.' He straightened his shoulders. 'I, Gianni Durante Carlos Bonmarito, ask you, Emma Grace Rose, to do me the honour of becoming my wife. Will you marry me?'

Emma felt tears sting her eyes. She cleared the tightness in her throat. 'Yes, please.' She blushed and tugged at his hand. '*Si. Grazie*, Gianni. Now get up.'

'So you have been practising for this moment?' It was his turn to tease as he stayed at her feet. 'Then I should have said it in Italian. *Vuoi sposarmi?*'

'In English was fine.'

She tugged again, and he stood up and lifted her back onto his lap and hugged her. She hugged him back and he felt so warm and solid and precious and she never wanted to let him go.

Then he reached into his pocket and produced a velvet box. 'It is bad luck to offer a proposal without the ring,' he said, and handed the box to her. 'This ring is my promise to marry you.'

When she opened it she gasped. On a satin bed lay an enormous white diamond, and she hesitated to even touch it. He lifted it from its bed and slid it onto her finger, and she wondered how he'd guessed the size right. But now wasn't the time to ask.

'Diamonds for the bride is an old Italian tradition,' he said seriously. 'We believe the flames of love fuel the intense heat that creates a diamond.' She felt the tightness in her throat thicken. But he wasn't finished. His voice dropped to a murmur.

'This diamond holds the future facets and joys of our life together.'

She gazed at the ring on her finger. Unable to believe he had proposed, and with such romance, at the end of such a crazy day. 'The ring is beautiful. And so was your proposal.'

'As a proposal should be. You are my world and I can wait no longer to keep you safe by my side.'

She snuggled in, one small cloud on her horizon. She needed to be near her parents, at least some of the time. 'And where shall we live?'

He stroked an errant blonde strand of hair tenderly off her forehead. 'Could you live in Italy some of the time, *cara*?'

'Wherever you go, my love.' She could. And Grace would enjoy the change. But Lyrebird Lake was her heartland.

'We will buy here. I have several properties on the lake lined up for your appraisal. Most of the year we will spend at your lake but there will be many journeys to teach our children their dual heritage. And I will teach them how to cook authentic Italian cuisine.'

She could see it. He understood. She should never have doubted him. Perfect. She sighed. How had she been so fortunate to find a man who made all her dreams come true?

His voice lowered. 'I hope you do not mind if we marry as soon as I can arrange for it.'

CHAPTER TWELVE

GIANNI didn't just arrange the wedding—he created the occasion he deemed essential for his bride.

The reception was held at the Lakeside, in the gardens beside the lake. Gianni hired the entire complex and a wedding planner to create a joyous and authentic Italian wedding that touched the hearts of all romantics who lived in Lyrebird Lake. And brought an incredulous smile to Gianni's brother Leon's face when he flew in for the wedding.

Gianni's young nephew looked debonair as he danced with Grace, flower girl and flower boy bringing more smiles to the faces of the guests.

Leon danced with Tammy, Emma's bridesmaid, and watched with a lightening heart as he saw his son's first spontaneous smile since his mother's passing.

Musicians with piano accordions played gaily while guests danced and silver bags of almonds and biscotti favours with the bride and groom's photograph emblazoned were handed out as wedding mementoes for the guests. Gianni forgot nothing. And the huge multi-layered Italian wedding cake, topped with the traditional figures of the bride and groom, impressed Grace the most.

Gianni's new daughter fell in love with the cake, and such was her delight that Gianni had a tiny version created for her Barbie house so that she could have weddings galore with her friends.

After discussion with Emma and Rex, Gianni arranged for Emma's parents to move from Brisbane and back into the family home. He'd secured the services of two sisters and their husbands as twenty-four-hour carers, all trained and empathetic in the care of the disabled, for Clare. Never again would Emma have to worry that her mother was unhappy away from her home.

The house was adjusted to make it easy for Clare to be cared for, and Rex could return to the town and friends that he'd grown up with. They too shared the joy of their daughter's wedding without the responsibility of keeping Clare safe and happy.

Late on the night of their wedding, the newlyweds stood on the deck of their isolated chalet, and gazed out together over the moonlit stillness of the lake.

In the distance Gianni heard the wind chimes as they pealed joyfully like the antique organ from one of the chapels in his homeland. As he cradled the warmth of his wife's slender hand in his he stared out at the starj24
filled sky and thanked God and the woman

beside him for the joyful turn his life had taken.

He pulled her back against his body, her softness like balm to his now quiet soul and the tiny bulge of her stomach firm beneath his hand reminding him of more fulfilment to come. He rested his chin on the top of her head and sighed deeply as the last of the tension dropped from his shoulders.

'We must have chimes in our new home,' he said, 'I find such pleasure when the breeze stirs them.'

Emma turned in his arms and smiled before she leaned up and kissed him with a teasing promise of more. 'There's no wind, my love. It's our lyrebird bringing his wedding gift to us. Our own special lyrebird to keep us safe for the future.'

'*Cara mia, ti voglio bene*,' he said in Italian as his heart swelled. 'My darling, I love you.'